TO THE BARD
with great love.

Chapter One

Her golden hair tangled in his fingers. Pressing so close, his human heart beat softly, softly against her dewy, silken skin. Though the afternoon sun hung in the sky, the inside of their tent was dark as night. A lone flickering candle lit their bed.

She stared at this man, feeling both whole and empty, desperate to be with him, terrified he might leave. His eyes were closed as he rested in divine exhaustion. She could stare forever at his lashes as they curled, at his chestnut-colored locks, at his dusky cheek with its closely shorn beard. At him.

She rarely took a mortal lover, but this

prince had appeared in her stronghold as if magicked to her. She was drawn to him inexplicably. His words enflamed her. His presence sweeter than a gift of milk and honey. She could not imagine eternity without him.

She nuzzled against his chest, as if to memorize its scent and the feel of his sweat on her lips. She whispered with a smile, "I would think you had goals of ensnaring me for my throne if we were not both so aware it cannot be passed to another."

The man's laughter rumbled in her bones as he kissed her brow. "Nay, it is only you I desire, Queen Mab."

"You have a taste for those above your rank?" She halted his answer before he could make one and asked, "Or needs your appetite be whetted more?"

"Whetted more and we shall be wedded for sure, my faerie queen," he replied, lifting his soft hand to trace her jaw line from ear to chin. "The dreams you bring at night pale in comparison to these moments which heat the day."

His eyes flickered at a sound outside their room.

Mab heard it, too.

Horse hooves and clanging bits of metal, and large numbers of both. A cry came from the outskirts of the camp. She sat straight up as her prince threw on his tunic and ran to the door.

"I shall return," he promised.

Queen Mab nodded. The sounds of battle were coming closer.

She cursed as she rose, grabbing her wrap in case she had need to fly. Her prince insisted upon this voyage to bring her white bull to the holy spring of Bandusia. He vowed their travels would be safe and smiled upon by the very gods themselves.

But as she thought upon it, it seemed puzzling that the gods would care. It was then that she wondered why it seemed so important to remove the bull from the safety of her realm in Verona in the first place.

The world slowed.

It suddenly seemed quite a strange action to take. Why had she listened to this man? She looked out where her prince exited and suddenly realized that despite sharing the road and a bed and her heart, she did not know his name.

Awakening struck her like a lightning bolt as the spell lifted, tearing away all artifice. Queen Mab rushed out of her tent, flinging open the flap. The sun hung like an orange coal, the soot and haze masking the sky in a cloud of death. Cries filled the air as her camp fell under attack. Her soldiers were too busy engaged in hand-to-hand with the enemy to notice what had been taken.

This, all of this, was a diversion to hide the theft of her sacred bull.

Two men ran along the horizon with her animal in tow. Their cloaks were as dark as midnight, but night cannot hide in the day. Shadows become silhouettes. It would have been better to dress as fire, for she saw them just as clearly.

Cloven hooves and woolly legs peeked out from beneath the robes of the man who had once been her prince. He cared no longer for secrecy. His disguise had melted away, revealing his true face, horns and all. He even paused to look back, to see her standing there his fool. He threw her a kiss and smiled.

"Faunus," she swore.

She knew him of old. As she was the ruler of dreams at night, he was the lord of those at day. He spent the hours between sunrise and set frolicking in the fields, playing the siren song of his pan pipes with no heed to their consequence, his loins always the master.

Two demigods of light and dark, she and he. She had thought Faunus a tenuous ally. They found understanding in one another, sympathy for the burden and toil of shaping man's idle thoughts.

She laughed when he'd gotten into mischief in centuries past, but this was too far. Once content to woo women by the stream, it now appeared his sport was to woo a queen. But he did not think her a queen on his board, only a pawn in his game of political chess. Mab recognized Faunus's partner in this crime, a lord of the mortal realm from the house of Montague. This lord came to her many times to beg the stud of this sacred bull, an animal who sired only cows, cows whose milk quenched hunger and bestowed their drinkers with unnatural strength.

Queen Mab clutched her robe against her bare skin. Faunus had probably whispered words of power and glory to the foolish Montague, covering his eyes with a gauze of paper promises. This lord did not know his conquest was nothing more than idle distraction to Faunus, something to stave his boredom. This lord did not know the war he started with his sly thievery, thinking it could be forgotten by time or forgiven in the passing years. He did not know what he meddled with when he chose to meddle with her.

Her rage boiled to a fury as bright as a thousand suns.

Mab would educate him.

From every foot soldier fighting alongside Faunus to that lord from the House of Montague and every child he sired beyond, they would all pay dearly for the insult for as long as her immortal blood ran hot in her veins.

"Believe you so clever to escape Mab?" she roared as they ran. "You shall die begging for relief! You cannot hide from me!"

They would learn that, unlike Faunus with his empty threats and playful distractions, Queen Mab meant every word.

Chapter Two

"Who are they upon that plain?" Mab asked. The faerie captain peered into her scrying ball.

Though they were leagues away, the glass showed an army camped on the ridge of a hill. The valley below lay wasted, ash and brown, strewn with the broken bodies of friend and foe alike. Two men, one fair, one dark, took their leave from the amassed troops, perhaps in council or strategy or gossip, but two men who walked alone together among the dead.

"Lord Montague and his sworn brother, Lord Capulet. Often it is said that this man is dearer to his heart than life itself," the captain replied.

Lord Capulet reached over to grip the arm of the other man in friendship, as Lord Montague seemed to lean towards him for support.

"Is that so?" stated Queen Mab, her thoughts rife with the true damage she could fashion for this pair.

True, she could use her armies to decimate them. The death at these lords' feet was proof of her might. Every night, she slipped inside the Montague tents unseen. There, she hunted down Faunus's forces one by one, plaguing their dreams with such terror that they woke exhausted and fell in battle like straw before a raging fire.

Faunus had countered, seeing her hand at work in their minds, and warned his men to keep nocturnal hours with the owl and the wolf, to sleep within the safety of the sun. Some followed. But all men must sleep, especially those who had been kept awake all day by the nuisance of Mab's forces.

But how much more biting, how much more just, to turn Lord Montague's one comfort into an assassin's blade? To bait one against the other and in doing so, leave them to face the fight alone? Cruelty would be her weapon. She would wound their hearts as her own had once been shattered.

She would turn these friends, these Capulets and Montagues, into bitter enemies. She would make this Capulet her ally. How many more men would slip into the arms of rest if she had a human who could fight when her strength was at its weakest, a mortal with as much to lose as she? A satisfied smile stretched across her face—the House of Capulet would do fine. She would ensure they never aligned themselves with the visions of Faunus again, that for generations when the name Mab crossed the tongues of conversation, their children would quake with fear.

She looked once more into her scrying ball and saw the days to come — the betrayal, the revenge, and the fall of these two Houses. The truth of their future would be the meat on the hook she cast. Whether she was the catalyst that caused these tomorrows or this turning merely fulfilled their destinies, she was happy to play her role.

The captain shifted uncomfortably in Queen Mab's silence. He knew better than to speak. Neither moved until campfires dotted the darkened horizon. Then, she cried to her faerie host, "Bring me my chariot!"

It was brought forth by two fairies the size of butterflies. The hazelnut was harnessed with spider web to two insects smaller than sight. Grasshopper wings made the roof, spider legs made the wheels, and a cricket leg the whip to speed her steeds. She waved her hand and in a spiral of smoke, Mab became no larger than a jewel upon a signet ring.

She climbed aboard and flew into the sky. Sailing over her army, she made way towards the enemy camp. Who would pay mind to an invasion the size of a moth? Not those soldiers who stood watch. Soon, they found their eyelids heavy. As they succumbed to sleep, she drove over their throats, making their dreams nightmares of blades and blood.

She landed by the tent of Lord Capulet. The guards at his door did not bother to look down as she crept inside the flap. Lord

Capulet rested on his bed, his oil lamp still burning in case he had need to rise in the middle of the night to take arms. He was barely eighteen, almost halfway through his mortal life, and still without a beard. There was a time not long ago when man worshiped the gods and knew the secrets to see a century or more. But now they locked the doors on knowledge, they cowered inside the darkness of their fears, and most would die before four decades had risen and set before their puny eyes. She pitied them.

Lord Capulet's dark, olive coloring spoke of his southern ties, unlike the fair skin and blonde hair of the Montague she sought to destroy. Their heritage had never crossed, and so long as she could play her hand, they never would.

As she regarded him, she thought that if he had not aligned himself with someone willing to commit such an atrocity against her, to make a fool of her and her heart, she might have been charmed into filling such a head with sweet dreams. But the time for such things was done and this man would not escape her nightmares. There would be no peace in this house. Enmity sewn would not be unthreaded. Nay, it would be woven into the very warp of the Houses of Capulet and Montague, and any hoped-for happiness destroyed with the shuttle she slid through the fabric of this man's mind. It would have been a pleasure to bring dreams of peace to someone after six months of terror, she reflected, but tonight would not be that night.

She pointed her rosewood wand and the lamp went out, plunging him into darkness and feeding her power. Cloaked from view in these shadows, she waved her wand once more and brought forth the cloud of smoke to return her to the size of a human woman.

"Lord Capulet," she murmured.

He stirred and whispered, "Hmmm?"

"A great disservice has been done to you and yours. The House of Montague seeks to destroy your home, to annex your lands, to undo the work of your fathers," she spoke. She planted a dream of such reality that in the morning, he would believe it prophetic and true.

"Pull down the House of Montague," she whispered. "Destroy them before they destroy you. Raise your sword and strike down the liar who falsely professes to love thee."

Lord Capulet stirred in his sleep, her words slowly catching on. The poor man's legs moved as if he ran. He thrashed as if he could escape her touch.

"But why?" he whimpered.

"Because," she replied as she leaned over and whispered in his ear, "I have seen the days to come, my Lord Capulet, and have seen the destruction that will be wrought by the House of Montague." She let his dreams reflect the future of that which might be. "Strike. Strike now with fierce determination and cut them like wheat before the reaper. Tear them out by the roots so that their weeds will not choke the last of your family, leaving your line barren, withered, and dying upon the vine. I have seen what the fates have in store, Lord Capulet. Your House shall be slain by the hand of Montague, and the sin shall be yours if you do not banish them from your heart and from the hearts of all your offspring."

He tossed in his bed, his brow furrowed. Queen Mab breathed out the dream, let it settle on his eyes to cloud his vision and keep him from seeing anything beyond.

"Smite them where you find them. You and your children shall always have an ally in Queen Mab, a queen who will owe you a debt. Remember."

"Remember..." he murmured as his body descended into the reality she had molded just for him.

She stepped away. Only the morning would tell if her message had struck his heart true. And if it did not, if he did not at once begin the beat of the war drums until the very earth shook in time to their thrum, she would visit him every night until his answer changed and he was powerless to say no.

₧ℂ

She did not have to return the following night, for standing upon the same plain where just the day before they joined in friendship, Lord Capulet turned his army against Lord Montague, crying, "Never shall our Houses be joined!"

Though the war was not yet won, the taste of one so easily turned was victory sweet upon Mab's lips.

Chapter Three

The battle-scarred land was as gray as the sky. The wind swept across the soot-covered countryside, the grasses bowing to their mistress. Though the battles had been senseless, the bloodshed great, over the years Mab began to see war's appeal. She sculpted the world into a living nightmare. Never before had so many welcomed her nightly embrace, praying for her dreams to take them away. But even so, the play had grown tiresome, her boredom great. Tonight she would bring the final act and hereafter find different amusements to pass the days.

A single owl, brown and mottled as tree

bark, flew across the clouds to Mab's outstretched hand. He lit softly upon her slender wrist, jumping to her shoulder where he could nibble her hair in false affection in the hopes of a bloody treat.

"My queen," spoke a soldier dressed in charcoal.

She did not bother to turn towards Lord Capulet's man.

"Queen Mab," the man continued, kneeling before her in the dust. "I delivered the draught. Lord and Lady Montague are abed."

She looked up at the fortress, at the gates which these foolish mortals thought they could keep barred from her. In the passing months, Lord Capulet had driven the Montagues back until finally the Montagues retreated to this building of stone where they stayed, cowering under siege.

She smiled an icy smile at the soldier. "And how shall I repay you for your service?"

The soldier did not lift his eyes, but stared down at the ground. "Truly my queen, I live to serve."

She stepped closer, her dress made of a

thousand cobwebs, spun by a thousand spiders, rustling as she walked.

"Indeed, I have allowed you to live in order to serve. But your queen is feeling generous. Tell me, soldier, of the longings of your human heart."

He stammered as his wall of secrecy crumbled, "Perchance to dream..."

She ran her finger along his collarbone. The owl upon her shoulder cried.

"And what dream would you like to live as though it were real?"

"I should like to be brave," said the soldier. "Brave and strong..."

She smiled.

"...with a lovely wench at my side."

Her back stiffened, but her expression never changed. "You shall have all that and more."

She waved her hand. A look of peace and tranquility fell upon the soldier's face before he faded into slumber. She held out her hand and a wisp of smoke escaped her fingertips, entering the man's nose as he inhaled, traveling to his mind to fill it with the world he so desired.

But before she withdrew, she touched his lips. "Think that you can yearn for another while a queen stands before you? Think you that I am so grateful for your report that I would tolerate a rebuff from a beast such as you? Nay, soldier." Where she touched, she left angry boils and sores to repulse any woman who might look upon him. "You take too many liberties. I know what lies in the dreams of man. Indeed, I am the one who placed them there. But if your queen stoops to grant you a favor, and you chose to serve your animalistic lust, you may be sure you shall be cast down to your rightful place among the creatures of earth and offal. You may be sure."

She turned to her army of faerie folk. "Watch him. See that he rests in pleasant slumber. If he does not wake up in a day or a year or a century, who would miss such a soldier?"

Her faerie companions laughed and settled beside the man.

Queen Mab tossed her owl into the sky. As

he fell, she shrank and transformed. The bird caught her upon his back as he swooped and they took off to the tower where the Montagues slept.

"Prepare for my return!" called Mab from the heavens. "Soon we shall feast!"

Her faerie host cried out in response, their voices raised as one in the lust of war.

Chapter Four

True to the word of the soldier, the castle was asleep. The owl flew to a window ledge high above the parapets. Mab dismounted and entered the room with its fur bedding and carved furnishings. The fair-haired Lord Montague slept with his wife curled upon his chest.

How fitting would be her revenge! What better way than with love? Lord Montague would worship her alone, Mab thought. She would ensure it. She would use his own heart to control him, to destroy him like he and Faunus colluded to destroy her. He would rue the day he ever fought beside the god of daydreams.

Mab waved her wand and was at once full size. She peered into a looking glass hanging on the wall. She wondered what form she would take in these coming dreams. Mab waved her wand and the tendrils of smoke entered the man's nose.

It was a dream of home and hearth. A hunting dog ran in from the fields and Lord Montague entered a cottage with his sword strapped to his side.

"Wife!" he shouted. "I have returned!"

Mab turned, knowing that he saw his beloved in her face. She wiped her hands upon her apron and smiled at the man. "I have been waiting for you," Mab replied.

She filled the house with the smells of sugar and spice. She cloaked herself in longing and comfort, feeding the flames of his passion until his desire was so tangible, she could swim through it like water.

Yet, he paused, unsure, as if he could sense her lie. The hair on the hound's back stood, a growl rippled from his throat.

"Begone," Lord Montague replied.

His single word was a slap.

Her eyes flashed as his stinging authority struck her illusion, threatening to tear it away.

But she steadied it. And then she smiled. She was the Queen of Dreams, not some wandering fancy of the mind. No human would tell her how to shape her worlds. Mab let the house decay into nightmares, the walls melt with screams. She was the only light in this tomb. She reached for Lord Montague, her arms outstretched to gather him in.

"Love me," she commanded. She drew him towards her. Her arms wrapped around him and grasped him tight. The sky boiled as he struggled.

"You will love me," she commanded again.

But he did not listen. Instead, the man's form began to shift, to writhe and twist. The house returned to normal. Lord Montague morphed into a figure which she had not shaped.

Queen Mab stepped back.

His hair began to grow until it hung past his waist in terra cotta curls. His face became more delicate. His clothing strained against the soft curves of his new body. Beside him, his hunting dog's tail spread and grew until it fanned out into the blues and greens of a peacock, his fur replaced with feathers, his snout grown into a beak.

Queen Mab hissed like a cat. "Juno."

As her clothing changed to the golden robes she wore when appearing in corporeal form, the Roman goddess gave an acknowledging smile.

"Queen Mab," she greeted, the ice in her voice as cold as the daggers of winter.

Mab knew the pretense was useless and with a wave of her hand returned to her garments of black, which clung to her body and hinted at her wicked delights.

"To what do I owe this pleasure?" Queen Mab asked.

Juno stepped further into the home and looked around, her peacock familiar following her footsteps wherever she walked. "I suppose for some a place like this is their heart's desire. It is strange that you would be drawn to such a mortal, though. It seems beneath you."

Faunus stepped into the room. His eyes met Mab's and she knew exactly what led Juno to interfere.

Mab stated with contempt, "This mortal, Lord Montague, stole a bull of mine."

"And that was enough to start a war?" Juno replied, mockery coloring her words. "My, I was not aware you were so fond of the bovine..."

"I do not take kindly to theft."

"And I do not take kindly to creatures such as yourself tearing asunder a true love match I have carefully orchestrated for the sake of some bullish affection," Juno snapped with flashing eyes.

"Do not threaten me," spat back Queen Mab. "May I remind you that we are in the land of dreams and that this is my domain?"

"But you use your domain to influence one who comes under my protection and so," Juno replied, "I have come to defend him."

The peacock spread his tail and let out a fearsome cry.

"If you needed a bull," Juno continued, "You need only to have asked and I would have provided you with one."

Queen Mab laughed, "I have no use for Jupiter."

Juno stretched out her hand. Though she stood across the room, Mab felt as if ropes of fire were wrapping around her throat, closing in tighter and cutting off her breath. She instinctually reached up, knowing full well that they were not there.

Juno smiled. "My dear woman, you may control the world of dreams, but I control the land of the living and at this very moment, my hands are wrapped around your bodily throat."

"I am immortal. I do not fear death," said Mab dangerously.

"There are things much worse than dying, my foolish, power-hungry child," replied Juno. "You came here to claim this mortal man's heart, which, I am afraid, I cannot allow."

Queen Mab ceased her struggling and for the first time, a chill ran down her spine.

"Despite your power and tricks, I find you quite repulsive," spoke Juno. "That seems a fitting way to spend the centuries that you must endure. Indeed, quite a fitting punishment for someone with a heart so vulgar and impure."

Juno stepped close to Queen Mab, circling her as her peacock drew a wider circle beyond. Queen Mab could feel the power that Juno was drawing up through the earth, through the barriers of the dreamscape, to weave her spell.

"You shall be confined to darkness and cold, to visit people only in dreams. No longer shall you meddle in the affairs of man. No longer shall you move with the freedom that you do. No, you shall live until you have learned the lesson of the act you have tried to commit. You shall live forever locked up in night, never to feel the warmth of the sun, never to feel the companionship of another, since it seems quite clear you are incapable of bearing this responsibility.

"In your mirror, you shall look quite the same, but you shall be an illusion to any that cast their eyes upon you. They shall see a face that matches your heart, as vile as it may be. Once revered for your beauty, you will instead reflect your true nature. Like your dreams, reality shall shift to display the secrets of your dark soul. This prison is of your own making, but I gladly forge the bars of justice to hold you."

With that, Juno released Queen Mab. Mab collapsed upon the floor, gasping for breath.

"The funny thing about dreams, Mab, is that they fade so quickly upon waking. Indeed, I should be surprised if you have any memory of this conversation at all. You shall wander the earth and never know why all manner of people step away when you enter the room, no idea why you should repulse them so. I believe this is a fitting punishment for your crime. You shall never know love unless your own heart changes, a task I am sure you are quite incapable of."

Juno walked to the door, her robes sweeping the floor with each step. Her peacock flanked one side and Faunus the other. Before they left, Juno gave Mab a sideways glance, her shoulders shivering with repulsed delight. She whispered to Faunus. "My, my. Quite as repugnant as I have always suspected."

She swept out the door and called from the yard, "Your bull shall be returned tomorrow!"

Faunus gave Mab a wink. "This has all been a most amusing diversion."

And then the dream faded to reality.

Queen Mab found herself standing alone in an empty room with two sleeping figures in a bed. Her owl still waited on the window sill.

Her mind tried to piece together the memory of the dreamscape. It felt like catching raindrops. The thoughts slid through her fingers and were gone. Only one image stayed in her head. She had been successful in securing the return of her bull.

Nothing else remained.

She would return home tonight, leaving the Capulets and Montagues to play out whatever end they wanted to this game of war. She had won, and that was all that she desired. She looked in the mirror and admired her face in the glass. Such a face could stop men in their tracks, she thought before she left.

Chapter Five

Queen Mab stood before her dressing table. She had flown upon her owl to her palace outside Verona, overwhelmed with the satisfaction of victory. Her estate stood untouched from the ravages of the war, its topiary gardens tended by the faerie folk, her home of gold and butter colored marble gleaming from their ministrations. Her palace existed in a space which could only be found by those who sought her by name, only seen by those who knew what was already there. But she knew that no one would trouble her tonight. For the first time since the war began years ago, there would be no dreams. She called to her faerie attendants. "Come! Prepare my bed!" she cried.

With a rustle of wings, her two handmaidens entered her room, chattering and giggling as they came.

Queen Mab did not look over her shoulder as she felt their hands untie the laces, their nimble fingers freeing her from the vice of daily dress.

"Tomorrow shall be a celebration," she pronounced. "The war is ended! My sacred bull returned! And all our people can look forward to returning home after ages of this mortal bloodshed."

Her ladies murmured in excitement.

"Tell the house to prepare for the feast!" Mab stated as she turned.

The two fairies recoiled as she met their eyes, stumbling back as if to get away from her.

"What is the matter?" Mab asked. When they did not answer, but continued to stare, she looked about the room wildly for the thing that frightened them.

The one faerie whispered, "Have you

looked into the mirror, my queen?"

Mab turned and saw nothing but her face. "What? You act as if there is something wrong."

"You do not see?" said the other.

"No," replied Mab. Her heart became cold as she saw her handmaiden's fear turn from fright to disgust. "Is this some mean trick?"

"We must away," said the first. "We must tell the house to prepare for the feast without delay."

The two flew out of the room like the hounds of hell themselves were nipping at their heels, glancing back as they left as if to see if they were pursued. Mab looked again in the mirror.

"They think to make the fool of me," she hissed. "Perhaps that Faunus has corrupted their minds. I shall not tolerate disloyalty in my own handmaidens. Tomorrow, I shall seek their replacement."

But on the morrow, when the first mote of sunlight fell upon the room, her handmaidens came in to wake her as they had always done, only they behaved as if they could not see her.

Though they could hear her voice, they searched high and low for their missing queen, thinking it some sort of game. Her shouts and screams only elicited giggles, her demands brought their playful remarks. Mab drifted restlessly through the house, watching the preparations for the feast, and yet no glance fell her way, no object moved at her touch.

Then she stepped into a sunbeam.

Verona dissolved. Her eyes opened and she awoke as if from a dream. She was once again in her bed. She sat up, startled, and looked around. It was her room, but it was as quiet and as cold as a tomb. Her breath came out in frozen clouds. Icicles hung from the corners of her dressing table and dripped like wax from her sconces and chandeliers. She called for her handmaidens, but her voice echoed down the empty hallways and no one replied.

She touched her skin, her hair, the bedclothes, a hairbrush. She was real and so was this world. She tried desperately to remember what means of witchcraft had been practiced upon her, but the dream of the night before, from the moment when she was in Lord Montague's home to the moment she departed upon the back of her owl, was gone in a haze of forgotten memory.

Her naked feet padded her way across the biting marble stones to her balcony. She opened the doors. The sky was dark, without a single star, and the world covered in snow. No footstep of man or beast marred the blanket of perfect white. She called out again to the world, hoping for some sign. Silence was its response.

She tried to shrink her form, to call for her chariot to take her away. But she held no more power than an ant telling an elephant to bow before it.

She had been banished from the touch of day.

Terror gave way to anger. She stormed through her empty palace. It was as if it was frozen in time with her as its prisoner. She dashed objects of beauty upon the floor and walls, treasures she had spent years gathering like a magpie. But no amount of screams or sobs, destruction or threats changed her situation. Mab sat once more upon her bed. She was trapped. There was no escape.

Exhausted and emotionally wrought, she lay her head upon her pillow and closed her eyes.

And then she opened them.

She was once again in her Verona. She looked around the room and it was as she always knew it. The cold was gone, the sounds of the house filled her ears. That tomb of white was now replaced with the warmth of gold gilt and candlelight. She rose and ran to her balcony. The sun had set and the stars welcomed her home. Her heart leapt with gladness, overflowing with gratitude for just a moment before it turned to bitter rage at this kidnapping.

She cooled its heat by telling herself it must have been a trick of the mind.

But her guests were arriving for the battle-won feast. Dragons and faeries, gnomes and dryads, they lined her garden and filled the night with raucous merriment. Now was the time for celebration!

Ready to put aside the strange dream and join in the festivities of her victory, she walked to the top of her grand staircase and looked down upon the ballroom of revelers. The crowd hushed. The horned and pointed faces of her faerie friends turning towards her. The dancing stopped.

But it was not in reverence.

Their alien black eyes widened with fear. Their bodies shrank. Nervous laughter tinkled across the floor.

Her mouth dried.

"The battle is won, my friends," she said with forced lightness. "You need not recoil. No favors shall I ask of you today, no commands shall spring from my lips. Tonight we celebrate!"

Their voices did not rise as one in support of her call. Instead, they backed away. They placed their goblets upon the tables and made carefully for the doors like prey creeping out of the den of a sleeping bear.

"You act as if I am a monster," she raged. Like a dam breaking, they ran. "Dare you to abandon your queen?" she cried as she flew down the steps. Their voices screamed in terror and cried out in fear.

Her faerie captain, one she once thought a dear friend, fell to his knees gibbering and pleading. "Oh vile creature! Spare me my life!"

Something, some soft part of the last remains of her heart, broke. She roared as he scrambled away. "A vile creature you say? Very well! So you shall have!"

She chased them from her hall, chased them from her house, chased them all away until the only fear and laughter came from the repeated memories still ringing in her ears.

As she looked out upon the rising moon, she thought she saw the silhouette of a goat man and heard the drifting melodies of a joyous, piping tune.

Chapter Six

"Quite happy, they are," whispered Juno, looking down upon the couple as they gazed upon their son.

The birthing room was still shuttered in darkness. Though the crisp chill of fall nipped the air outside, the heat in this room from the fire caused sweat to prickle upon Lord Montague's brow. Exhausted, his wife lay upon the pillows of her bed as her midwife bathed their wailing child, unaware that this birth was witnessed by the gods.

Faunus played a bored trill upon his pipes.

"Are you so weary of this world that you can no longer appreciate the joy of hearth and home?" asked Juno with a smile.

"I have never appreciated the joy of hearth and home, goddess."

Juno laughed, "You are not one to mince words, are you, Faunus?"

"Mince steps, perhaps, but never words," Faunus replied.

"Look upon them," said Juno. "Look at the progeny of a century of planning."

Faunus stroked his beard, looking closer with a whisper of unfeigned interest, "I see now why you brought me here. This is the son of the son...?"

"Yes, of the son of the son of the couple you protected from Queen Mab. I have never forgotten their devotion to me, and indeed, generations of their family have not forgotten either."

"You chose wisely," Faunus complimented.

"The House of Montague is strong. The strength of the gods beats within their veins. Their protection was well worth the price of that sacred bull you stole, is it not, Faunus?"

Faunus shrugged. "But to what end, Juno? At what cost is this child? More than just the bull which you took after it was rightfully won by me."

"Relinquishing that bull secured this House."

"I care not for politics and babes."

Juno's eyebrow rose as she looked over at Faunus. "My... a century has almost passed and yet do you still mourn the loss of your queen of dreams?"

"I would not say mourn," replied Faunus. "But do you not miss the way my people might ride through both day and night? Do you not miss the taste, the hunt, the flavor that she brought to the darkest moments of this world's turn?"

Juno looked back at the family. "Do not feign affection. You do not miss her presence, old friend, despite what your lips might say. Your lips were always the better for silencing than speaking, so speak it plainly or do not speak at all. "

He leaned forward. "Ah, Goddess Juno, as perceptive as you are wise. I should have known better than to think I could deceive you." He motioned to the window, at the cracks of light yearning to contaminate the room. "Worry has indeed begun to trouble my days. I think perhaps that Mab shall grow weary of the night. I know her well. She shall grow tired of her prison. I fear she shall seek to overthrow thee."

Juno laughed, "A goddess fearful of a queen? You have spent too much time in the courts of man. Mab is defanged. She is as toothless as this newborn babe whose bite relieves his nursemaid's aching and swollen breast."

"You made a castrato of her for a breeding pair of Montagues. Think you that a demigod takes such an insult as a lesson? Think you that this education makes her hold her power less dear?"

Juno smiled like a cat with cream. "She shall learn to love or learn to love her prison, and whichever she chooses makes to me no difference."

"Heed my warning!"

"I hear you, Faunus, and shall decide myself how ominous the sky."

"The clouds hang black and heavy with

the storm."

"And perhaps they shall blow through. Now, hush. It is the time of naming."

The mother rocked her newly born child and whispered to her husband, "Romeo. I name thee Romeo."

Juno nodded in approval. "It is a good name."

The mother passed the child off to the nursemaid and settled back against her pillow. Her husband pressed his lips against her brow and left the room.

Faunus raised an eyebrow at the cold that had fallen upon the couple. "The winter follows the autumn harvest, I see. Perhaps we should have kept the bull."

Chapter Seven

Outside Mab's window, the rolling hills of Verona were covered in a deep layer of frost gleaming in the moonlight. The chamber in her palace was just as cold, the grey stones of this room icy to the touch. As she breathed, a cloud of white spoke the direction of her words.

The winter months of Italy brought her the most delight. The days grew short and the hours that her feet might tread the earth grew long. The cold was like a kindred reflection. It matched the distant chill that had taken up residence in her heart, that unending fear of walking in the sun and waking in a world where lonely powerlessness went on without end.

But here in Verona she ruled the night and gladly kept the darkness as her friend. Rarely did she have visitors. Indeed, most mortals were too fearful to seek out her council. And rightly so. She was not moved by pity or desperate stories in need of her compassion. Her price was hefty and rarely could a man afford the bill.

Even so, there was a man before her here in her mortal dwelling. A man who had found the path to her palace, and so must have sought her directly by name. This man knelt as he rightfully should before her slippered foot. He seemed to recoil every time he looked up at her face, casting his eyes to the ground, as if overwhelmed by the power he saw in her. It pleased her that he seemed knowledgeable of the rightful ways that one should address a faerie queen.

She smiled.

"Queen Mab," he murmured as he knelt before her, hand placed over his heart in fealty, if not devotion. "Forgive me for coming to you with a petition."

She thought for a moment, pausing to consider if she were in a mood for the dreams of man, so often tied to power and wealth. But perhaps he might surprise her. Perhaps he might give her a moment's distraction from the passing hours. She waved a slender finger so pale from the darkness of night, it looked like snow.

"My grandfather of old passed down the story that you were always a friend to our family, that your favor granted us special counsel and privilege," the man said.

Now he raised his eyes, eyes as brown as moistened loam to look at her, to plead. She descended from her throne and took the man's chin within her two fingers, turning his head this way and that. She sensed a regal bearing in his stance, in the way he pulled from her touch, as if not used to the hands of a stranger upon his face. The mark of Capulet still remained and reminded her of that foolish promise she had made to that ancestor of his.

"I seek out this friendship," he continued. "Please, guide my steps! Tell me how to move forward so that the House of Capulet may rise to greatness once again."

It was indeed always money or power. Mankind was so weary, Queen Mab thought.

"Indeed, your House has fallen quite from grace. What price shall you pay me to protect your House, Lord Capulet?" she asked.

"Anything. Anything!" he swore, gripping her fingers as if a lifeline.

She knew the truth. They would say "anything", but struggle and fight when she stated the recompense. She looked deep into his eyes, seeking out that which was held most dear. The answer came as quite a surprise. This man's greatest gift seemed to be his generous heart, his patient ways, and his loving spirit. So it should be hers to the envy of all.

"I shall take your kindness," she replied with a nod of her head.

Lord Capulet looked confused. "My kindness is freely given. Indeed, a boon of your choosing is yours to claim. Protect my

House and you may name the favor. If it is within my power, I shall grant it."

Mab smiled. "Indeed, you are kind."

She did not bother to clarify. She had proposed the price. He had agreed. Whether he was aware or not of the true meaning of her words was irrelevant. A bargain had been struck and the deal made. His kindness for her protection. She held out her hand to seal their contract. "Follow me."

He placed his hand in hers and she led the nervous man from the receiving hall to her laboratory. Seated upon the wall were small bottles filled with liquids, powders, and gases. She motioned to Lord Capulet to stay still inside a ring of wood inlaid into the floor.

She raised an empty jar and looked over at the gentleman.

Lord Capulet's eyes grew heavy and his head bobbed upon his neck like flotsam upon the sea. When he settled into stillness, she waved her hand. A pink cloud oozed from his pores, creating a halo of happiness around him. She waved her hand once again and the cloud drifted from Lord Capulet and into her glass. She placed a lid upon it. It was done. The world would worship her for this kindness and she could not wait to drink and watch as the populace knelt before her.

When Lord Capulet's eyes opened, there was a hardness that had not been there before, an edge to his words when he spoke. "How strange I feel..." he said, raising a hand to his brow. "I require a chair to rest upon."

"Nay," she whispered, "You must lie down."

He sank in the center of the circle as if lowered by pulleys and string. His eyes fluttered to half-mast as the dream overcame him. Mab watched it in her crystal ball. A young girl appeared. And a boy. And their meeting spelled disaster and the collapse of the House of Capulet.

As the last image faded, Lord Capulet's eyes opened. Slowly, he looked to Queen Mab for answers.

The words formed upon her lips and echoed through her chamber, as if the earth and stones about them joined in chorus to this prophesy. "Two households, both alike in dignity, in fair Verona, where we lay our scene, from ancient grudge break to new mutiny, where civil blood makes civil hands unclean."

"I do not understand."

Mab paused, then stated simply for him, "You shall soon have a daughter..."

"My wife is now with child..." he confirmed.

"You will name her Juliet."

"We had only spoken of names for my heir, but if a girl, I had thought of that name, Juliet..."

"Beware. She shall rise against you. If you wish for your House to survive intact, you must marry her off as young as her body can bear to a cousin, perhaps, or another from your own house."

Lord Capulet nodded.

"Then all shall be safe," Queen Mab said. Then she pointed at him. "Remember my words. This prophecy shall happen many years into the future and I am afraid that you will forget."

"Never, Queen Mab."

She inclined her head. "You are mortal and, as such, are subject to the failings of mortal minds and mortal hearts. I see that the House shall fall, which means that you will forget, that at some time during your sojourn on this earth, your feeble soul will be unable to resist the temptations of hospitality and good grace. If you wish to retain the House of Capulet, you must remember your hope lies with your daughter, and her betrayal will end your line."

Lord Capulet nodded. "I swear I shall remember, Queen Mab. I swear it all. Your knowledge is mighty and I am but a humble gentleman with human concerns of country and home."

Queen Mab leaned forward. "Indeed, your kindness preceded you. Now be gone."

As he left, she stared into the ball. The future was still shrouded in the haze of the million different missteps, but what she had said held true. Indeed, the house of Capulet would fall. She hoped the foolish lord remembered. She would hate to have to return her prize.

Chapter Eight

She flew in her hazelnut shell through the dark empty streets of Verona, enjoying the cold and knowing Lord Capulet's kindness waited in her pocket for when she finished her nightly ride. She wanted this one last journey before transformation—to view the world with her old eyes so that she might see the difference when she looked at it anew. Her chariot landed upon the branch of a tree. She leapt out, and before her feet touched the ground, she had returned to full human form.

"Whither do you wander, Queen Mab?" asked a voice from the shadows.

She would have recognized that voice from

anywhere. It caused fangs to grow from the center of her soul. Vengeance itself called to her to rip this creature into ribbons of meat.

She turned slowly. Standing beneath the torchlight and leaning against a stone wall was a horned, half-goat man. The shadows could not hide his form from her.

"Faunus," she acknowledged, icily.

He raised an eyebrow. "My, my dear queen. A century has passed and you still seem to be displeased at the sight of me." He gave her a wink and sauntered close. "You must admit, what we once had was most cunning sport."

She lashed out to rake his cheek with her claws, but he danced away before her fingers could make their mark.

"Now, now, is that any way to behave to one who held your heart so dear?" he laughed.

"It was a liar's trick," she spat.

"But a pleasant trick, and one which harmed you naught." He leaned forward. "Or did it? Was the heart of the mighty Mab so stolen that she would hold a grudge for nigh on one hundred years?"

She bit back her words, not giving him the satisfaction of a denial, nor the pleasure of the truth. Instead she said, "You stole nothing more than a bull."

"...one which was returned to you..."

"And made me look the fool."

"Ah, no one can make you look the fool but yourself, Queen Mab. You have only yourself to blame."

She yearned to destroy him. Yearned to cast him into a sleep so deep that the world might end and he would still slumber in the arms of nightmares and ghosts. But she dared not, for fear of Juno's intercession.

And for the fact that the goat man spoke truth.

"Why do you trouble me, Faunus?" she asked, waving her arms to the darkness. "It is night and you should be abed so that tomorrow when the sun rises, you might rise to bed the virgins that you woo. What makes you trespass upon my domain?"

"Merely came to see how Queen Mab fared. I hear Titania is still having fits that you sold your sleeping potions to Oberon."

"He bears the blame for that mishap, not me."

"Indeed, what a cheerful Midsummer you arranged for such a forgiving king and queen."

"Quiet."

Faunus pulled out his flutes and played her a trill.

"Tell me true, what brings you here?" she asked.

Faunus shrugged. "Want of pleasant companionship?"

"The time of us keeping company is far behind us."

"But new friendship is in bloom. What say you we drink a cup of kindness?" asked Faunus with pointed interest.

Mab looked at him in disgust. "Of what do you speak?"

"I have just been forced to look in upon the birth of a human child. I must say I am more interested in the formation of such a creature than the end result. I come to find distraction from these horrific visions that my eyes should never have seen."

"That is not why you came, my enemy."

"True. You always knew me best, my Mab," he confessed. "I hear you stole a cup of human kindness and I would like a draught."

She wondered who had told him, the news being but hours old. There were spies in her midst and she would make sure they did not see the next sunrise.

"The kindness kept shall not kiss your lips," she replied.

"Lips for kissing might yet woo it out of you."

"The wooing that might have won was done long ago."

"A pity. It would not have done you harm. Perhaps a game, Mab, a wager for the taste of kindness sweet?"

Mab paused, his words arresting her for just a moment. His words held intrigue, a feeling she had not felt for a long while.

He gave her a wink. "Now, there is my Mab."

"I was never yours, Faunus."

"Perhaps a peace between us two, a wager that might rid you of me or cease our feral spitting, instead turning us into two fat felines which sit before the fire and lick."

"What sort of a wager might give us that?"

"A game between two Houses! A taste of Capulet kindness to two mortals. Champions in battle, handicapped by their hearts."

"Handicapped by their hearts?"

"Is that not what the heart is? A twisted weakness? A chink in the armor of strength? The only thing that keeps man from rising to the top, as he is held back by pity for his fellows?"

Mab leaned against the archway of the bridge and regarded this her foe. "If the heart is made so weak by such a human state, why do you desire a taste of it so?"

"Curiosity," replied Faunus.

"Curiosity killed the cat."

"Then let me be the king of cats," Faunus replied.

"Not for all your nine lives. Tell me, Faunus, true - why do you desire the kindness?"

Faunus gave her a sideways glance. "You take me not at my word?"

"I have known you lo these many centuries, Faunus, and I am not a fool."

"Aye, not a fool, but once my fool."

"And never again shall I dance at your feet for the prize of a laugh and a smile. Tell me, Faunus."

"For the sport! You used to need not a reason, our pleasure was bait enough to tempt the fates."

"I rather like seeing you in despair," replied Mab. "My answer is no."

Faunus leaned forward and let the words drip from his lips like honey. "What if the stakes were higher? What if the game was more than just a laugh and a smile?"

"And what might be my prize?"

Faunus paused, his answer like a treat on a hook. "Too long have the Houses of Montague and Capulet been the pawns of our game. Like chess, we moved the pieces about the table, perfectly matched knight-to-knight and rook-to-rook. Let us bring this tiresome game to an end. Clear the board of all but two pieces. A cup of kindness to these two to overtake each's king. One side Montague.

One side Capulet. Let us take this game to check and mate so that we might begin anew."

"Whoever shall bring down the other's House the victor?"

"One side shall rise and one side shall fall. Whoever wins inherits them all."

"And what if both shall live or die?"

"Such an end will be not done, for if that is the case, the game is not yet won."

Mab sat quietly as she thought.

"Come, Queen, you are as weary as me. Centuries it has gone on, you banished, me bored. We could finally enjoy the splendor of the day! Come. Join in the fun. Sit not in the dark and rage at the brightness. Agree to the game and be done."

Faunus looked at her with the eyes of one she had unknowingly been forced to love, with a heart that once beat for her. She found herself pulling out the kindness from her pocket. Faunus held up two vials.

"You thought of quite everything, did you?" she remarked.

"And where would we be if I had not? Carrying the kindness in our palms like a drinker at a fountain? Come, Mab! Dispense with it! Let our distraction begin!"

She removed the cork and spoke the words to cause a single taste to float to the containers in Faunus's hand. She then placed the lid back on tight and hid the kindness away as if frightened it might decide to struggle to free from her grasp and run home to its master.

Faunus held out the one vial to Mab, pausing so that his hand lingered on hers before releasing it.

"Let it begin," said Queen Mab as she turned away. "We shall see who emerges the victor."

Chapter Nine

Queen Mab placed her brush upon her dressing table and stared at herself in the mirror.

Tonight she would go to the palace of Prince Escales to seek out her champion and see what pieces now played in Verona's game of political chess. The prince's palace was one of forced neutrality, so all would be in attendance at this masquerade no matter what meddling they dabbled in during the day. A mask of deep blue, the silver edging sparkling in the candlelight, sat before her, whispering promises of anonymity and stealth. She could watch and wait, carefully choosing the champion who would at last bring an end to a House which had plagued her too long.

She walked over to her great white wardrobe and flicked through her gowns of dragonfly wings and foxtails before pulling out the mask's mate and her choice for tonight's dress. The overlay was slashed and cut, as was the fashion in all the best homes of Verona, and from beneath the midnight velvet and scrolling silver embroidery came the gentle glow of fireflies.

At once, the unseen hands of her dream-servants were upon her, tying and untying, straightening her laces and cinching her corset. These invisible companions, born from her own mind, were her handmaidens now. The days that another faerie would look upon her were long since gone, the memory of why still eluded her. A final tug, a smoothing swipe, and she was dressed. A servant handed her the mask. She placed it upon her face and looked once more into her looking glass. She was a stranger to herself. A woman in blue stared blankly back at her as the touch of her only companions faded and she was left alone once more.

She walked through her palace, her feet echoing upon the marble, and out into the garden where she and the moon often talked.

"Bring me my chariot!" she cried, and once more the dream-servants silently brought her that which she called for. There were no lusty shouts of joy as she took off into the night sky as there once were. Only the silence, which left her alone with her thoughts and new schemes.

Who to be her champion, she wondered. What thread to pull to cause the entire House of Montague to fall and the House of Capulet to rise in glory?

She settled upon the wall of Prince Escales's palace, the windows bright with torches and fire. Carriages pulled up before the front doors and elegant lords and ladies exited, their ribboned feet light upon the marble stairs. The palace was almost as lovely as her own. Almost.

With a wave of her rosewood wand, the cloud of smoke wrapped around her and Mab grew in size until she was the same as the humans milling about. She looked upon the crowds, judging them as she went. So strange to see them with their eyes open, with the movement of life showing their true character. This one too cruel. This one too kind. This one unattached and of no import.

And then the Montague's whelping, that dog of a son, Romeo, passed by, his hair shining like the sun of high day. The anger rose as fierce and as mighty as if his great-grandfather's betrayal was only yesterday. She reminded herself to still the raging storm. Cool patience would teach her how best to pierce his heart. He would soon be done.

She followed him into the prince's hall, keeping her distance but never letting him out of her sight. He paused as he was announced at the top of the ballroom's grand staircase, preening like a cock beneath the gaze of the gentry. Queen Mab slipped quietly by and into the sea of silk and damask. As Romeo paused, so she paused, too. She took a goblet from a passing servant and raised it to the strangers beside her.

"To what shall we toast?"

"To the return of the prince's kinsman!" said one.

"And to the return of beauty to this court!" said another, sweeping a bow to the lady beside him.

Mab forced a tight smile. There was a day when any man would have prostrated himself upon the floor when he looked upon Queen Mab. She wondered if perhaps her mask caused this one's senses to stray.

There was a great clanging of glasses and the entire company ceased its idle chatter to look up at Prince Escales, who stood at the head of his staircase with a man at his side.

"We welcome to Verona our kinsman, Mercutio, son to the cousin we hold most dear. Warrior and soldier, he returns to us after defending our interests upon the field of battle. I ask your hand in making him feel the warmth and comfort of our friendship." Prince Escales held up his wine.

"Mercutio," Mab murmured, tasting his name upon her tongue. A strange figure, thought Mab, as she watched this young hero stand comfortably before the throngs of fellows. He had such grace and beauty. His olive skin and dark, loosely curling hair spoke of his southern ties, yet as the company parted, there Mercutio was calling out to the fair-haired Romeo. Mercutio seemed a man able to walk between the worlds of politics, seemed a friend to any who took his hand. He carried himself with the casual assurance of one with nothing to prove, and in doing so, was the most powerful man in the room. Here was the strength she sought. It was him. Mercutio. She rolled his name on her lips once more.

Mercutio stepped forward and clasped Romeo to his bosom. "My friend of old, too long have I been parted from your company. Together we shall see the sites of your town and set our sights on the fairest visions Verona has to offer."

"Your spirit seems light, good Mercutio."

"Seeming seems to tell a tale much different than I hold within," he replied. "I have seen the horrors of war and have found living much more to my liking. So close to the brink of death, watching brothers and friends succumb to its embrace, I find myself no longer wishing to nibble at the scraps Fate drops from her table. No. I shall take my place at her side and gorge myself upon the sweetest meats she feeds me, sucking the juices from her fingers and rejoicing that someday, my belly might finally be full. This living is too short and each day a loss. It is too easy to slip into darkness, to surrender to the call of sleep. But this I know, the nightmares that wait do not disappear with the closing of my eyes. I must chase them away. And so I shall! I shall live! And living means loving, and to loving, I seek out you, Romeo, to show me the beds where I might find my comfort and the arms that will welcome me in."

Mab stepped away from these men as they plotted their conquests and she began to think. If he sought safety in a lady's arms, perhaps hers could be the safest home he ever longed for. She could keep him as her companion after the game was won, a thanks for his servitude. She regarded him. Such a passing could be a pleasure. She would begin with dreams, she thought. She would visit him in the night and see what his heart held dear. Then, as passions grew, she would appear before him in corporeal form, inviting him to her palace. Once there, she would ensnare him, keeping him glamoured until the appointed hour and moment of death had slid into time like so many hopes and passing fancies. He would be hers.

"Pardon," said a voice. It had a gentle carelessness to it, a rasp from too many hours joyfully awake. She turned, and there stood Mercutio.

Close, his eyes were green as a stormy sea, yet they smiled at her, looking upon her mask delighted and even more cheered by what might lie beneath. "Fair lady, you seem familiar to me. Have we been acquainted before?"

"Nay," she replied, a hunter captured in her own net. "I have not had that honor."

"Then let us become acquainted now. I am quite without a partner and you would be doing me a great kindness, a charity really, if you would join me in this dance."

Romeo behind him recoiled, as if he thought Mercutio had picked the foulest woman in the room. Mab stiffened, the knife of this boy's cruelty nicking her pride, the uncensored truth of youthful honesty cutting deep.

But Mercutio held out his hand and gave her a wink.

She placed her hand upon his and let him lead her to their place in the pattern amongst the other couples. She knew from his touch he did not see that which his friend held true. It should not have mattered, but she felt a strange softening in her chest, a warmth in her fingertips. It had been many years since someone willingly gave her a gift of small and gentle kindness.

"We are lucky to have revelers here at our gathering," he said as the fife and drum began to play. "And luckier still to have a woman such as thee."

"And how would you know? You have not seen me uncovered. I might be a monster or a witch," she replied.

He laughed. "I have always believed that

the monsters in a room such as this tend to wear the sorts of masks a person cannot see."

He intrigued her, Mab thought, this lord and soldier of the world. They parted as they exchanged partners, forming circles on a spoke, and then back again.

"You are light of foot, my lord," complimented Queen Mab.

"And you carry yourself as royalty... you still have not given me your name."

"Names hold power," she replied.

"Then give me a taste of power to hold over you."

"It is a secret, dear sir, and the better for you to taste anon."

"Withholding a morsel from the lips of starving man? It is cruel that you whet my appetite thusly," he said as they spun palm to palm.

"Nay, gentle sir, the pangs of hunger make the taste sweeter and sharpens the flavor as it spreads across the tongue."

They ended the dance face to face, close enough that she felt his breath on her lips. "If the tongue of your taste tastes half as much as the tongue of your wit, you will keep a man groaning from the rich banquet of your cunning." His eyes sparkled like her stars before he broke the spell and escorted her off the floor. He bowed. "I hope I shall see you again this evening and perhaps join hands again in another dance?"

"If nothing more, I shall see you in your dreams," she replied.

"Ah! Such promises! You make me long to leave this frivolous pageantry and find myself abed." He smiled before stepping away to bring Romeo to his side. "Romeo, come! Let me introduce you to the fair Rosaline!"

Mab watched as the two men wandered away to a blushing maiden, a wisp of humanity, a frail child who seemed as if she might break when the imperfect world stumbled and tripped away from what she believed its intended path. She listened while Romeo took Rosaline's hand and kissed it tenderly, as if such lips could win a heart with their attention. "Gentle Mercutio, keep you this woman for yourself? Or can you spare her for a turn upon the floor?"

Mercutio laughed and clapped him upon the shoulder, "Go to! Dance! Be light of foot and fly!"

The beauty was at once upon Romeo's arm, her airy laughter imperceptible above the sound of the swelling strings.

But this time, Mab did not follow her chosen enemy's son. Instead she watched Mercutio. With all eyes upon the dancers, his smile faded to sadness, and he himself into the shadows. He walked out onto the balcony, cup of drink in hand. He stared at the stars and she knew at once that look --- the lonely mask of one apart from all his brethren in the room. There was something about the darkness in his eyes that reminded her of the face she saw in the mirror.

Mab faded away, needing to allow the ice to harden her heart once more. Mercutio may have set in the thaw with his touch, but she could not allow him to melt it completely.

Chapter Ten

The party done and the revelers gone, Mab flew outside the home of the Montagues. She looked at the windows as their soft lamps winked out one by one.

She thought of Mercutio.

Could she so use him to ensure that some morning the light from these lamps would not return?

True, there was none better suited for this task. And yet... and yet... there was something... some strange sense of wonder which made her wonder if her champion was truly he. He had looked upon her unflinching. It was a reaction she had not seen in over a century. She had not known how much she had missed that gentle leaning in of another soul. What eyes did he see gazing back at him through her mask? Did she wish to strike at such kindness with cruel correction? To take such a rare soul and twist him into a mere tool for her ends? To show him that behind her mask was nothing more than the spiteful malice of her heart?

Strangely, she wanted him to know that she was more.

She did not allow herself the luxury of further reflection. The moon hung swollen in the sky and in but a few hours the sun would rise to take its place. The window to this house of Montague was open, the crack all she needed to climb inside.

She drew her coach to Romeo's bed and settled her unseen steeds upon his linen cover. There he slept, his tumble of curls upon his pillow and his sweet breath causing his chest to rise and fall. She alit from her carriage and stepped close to his brow. Which dreams to birth, she thought. Which pictures to fill this pretty head? Something sugary as candy, to paint the next day so warm and safe that she might catch him unaware? Or perhaps something dark to set his feet upon another path which he might otherwise shy away from. She smiled. Such havoc she could raise upon him, perhaps visions of maidens that would plague him for days, keeping his heart from whispering its gentle cautions.

"What would you wish to dream, my young man?" she asked.

His lips whispered a word. "Rosaline..." they seemed to say.

"Rosaline," she replied.

Romeo was no one extraordinary, just a lad like all the other boys in Verona, chasing skirts and fighting battles. If it was a Rosaline, if it was some girl by any other name... well, such dealings were never of any matter. This first move in the game was so easy, perhaps she would not even have need to consider Mercutio.

She turned back to Romeo. "Very well, boy, you shall have your Rosaline..."

He smiled.

"…but she shall not have you."

Mab climbed aboard her hazelnut shell and she flew off towards the window. Off to find this fair Rosaline and to fill her head with visions of quiet prayer and chaste ambitions, to encourage her to spur all things from a young lover such as Romeo.

Dreams were such fickle things. And the ambitions of the day made way for the ambitions planted at night.

Queen Mab would make sure of it.

Chapter Eleven

The final light in the prince's palace now went out, and Mab flew to where Mercutio's silhouette last fell. His window was open to the night air, as if he seemed to welcome anything the darkness might bring.

She landed her chariot upon his sill. She stepped into the room, returning to human size before her foot struck his bedroom floor. She waved her rosewood wand and at once the room was bathed in golden light.

He slept in a canopy of heavy red damask, but the curtains were pulled back to allow in the summer breeze. Though asleep, Mercutio's pulse beat as if he was being pursued, his body thrashed as if fighting some foe. His face was a book of stories much more complicated than even she could tell. She blew him a kiss which settled upon his heart and slowed its terrified beating. She knew it warmed his marrow and spread through his veins like the purring of a cat. She watched as his face relaxed and ceased its screwing, as he fell into gentle slumber and almost seemed to smile.

His lids opened slightly and his vision landed upon her.

She stiffened, her heart in her throat. When man or child looked upon her, half awake and half in sleep, they soon began to cry, to scream, to call for someone to banish a monster which had settled in their room.

"Who are you?" he asked.

She reminded herself that man was so feebleminded, so easy to sway. "One who cares to give you the world," she replied. He could be hers before the night was done. "What do you wish to dream of?" she asked.

"Power? Love? Happiness? Say the words and I shall chase the dark away."

"Of you," he whispered.

His answer took this queen of centuries aback. She regarded him for just a moment as she paused, remembering his kind touch from hours before. She had no reason to do it, but found her lips answering with her reply, "If that is what you wish to dream of, then so you shall have me."

She waved her rosewood wand and the tendrils of her smoke closed his eyes and silenced his mind.

At once, she was within, resting within a dark room made of stone, a prison cell with dripping horrors. Mercutio sat beside her, chained and in rags, weeping wounds marring his perfect flesh.

"Is this what you dream when you are left alone?" she asked.

He nodded, exhausted from the tortures he did bear, and pointed a manacled hand towards the door. "Soon the jailor will come in to begin the chase, a game of hide and seek with death at the finish line. It always ends with death."

Mab looked around the room, this landscape whose every color was a key to his troubled soul. "And have you seen this place in the world?"

"Aye," he said, his parched throat swallowing painfully. "It is where I was kept for a time, a place where I escaped from, and yet a prison to which every night I return."

"Then you must escape again," she replied.

His glassy eyes rose to rest upon her as she stepped forward fearlessly. She took her hands and placed them on his wounds. She touched the sores and scabs, these representations by his mind of the injuries no one could see. Whenever she passed, the skin was healed as if never destroyed by blemish. But deeper still, she cauterized the memories that brought forth these terrors in the night.

"The pain is gone," he murmured disbelievingly.

"All that and more."

The door to the prison opened and the jailor, a beast-like creature with jagged teeth and corded limbs walked into the room. His bloodstained nails were like daggers, his gray, scaly skin like armor. Mab pointed her hand at him, and in an instant, he was turned, shrinking until he was a kitten, playing and chasing after his tail until he danced off down the hall for adventure.

"You changed it," Mercutio said, blinking.

The shackles fell from his hands. Mab pointed to the walls and they exploded in a burst of starlight, filling the air with beauty, showing that just beyond the walls was a land of verdant green with rolling hills, dotted with olive trees. The sky was midnight and filled with the twinkling of the heavens. He stood, tears in his eyes and a mighty sob catching his words before he could speak.

"Is this your home?" she asked him.

He nodded. "From long ago. It is gone now, but, yes, this is where my happiest memories once were formed."

He stared at the night in wonder, a man dying of thirst realizing the mirage might not be a lie. He stepped forward, but before he went on, he reached back without a word and took Mab's hand in his.

"Dear lady," he said. His voice was breathless and he looked upon her as if espying a vision. "Art thou real?"

"What is real?" she replied.

His eyes burned into her heart as his breath quickened in his chest.

"Art thou true?" he asked.

"Indeed, my dear Mercutio," she answered. "I am truer than the blood which beats in your veins."

"Swear not by my blood, for it runs too warm."

"What else shall I swear by if not that which fuels your heart?"

"Swear by my heart itself which beats in constant rhythm, without which I would die."

"Then by thy heart, I do swear to thee that I am true."

They stood still, time ceasing its endless march for just a moment. He drew her in to his arms, full of weary gladness. Gently, he brought his fingers to her cheek and whispered, "Thank you," before sealing his gratitude with a tender kiss.

At once, Mab was back in his room, her breath stolen away. She looked at Mercutio resting peacefully.

Perhaps it was that weakness, that moment of shared connection that made her whisper the blessing, but she gave it. "I promise I give thee my protection. For as long as thou drawest air, I will fight the very heavens to keep thee safe."

He did not stir as her words settled upon him like frozen bits of glimmering starlight.

She stood back and felt an unwelcomed warmth, something that seemed to want to undo her strength and power. A wish to steal this man and leave another in his place.

She stopped her thoughts, swiftly chasing all softness away. She would need the most of her cruelty to seek the endgame that Faunus and she played.

She quietly left the bed chamber and made her way to the rooms beyond. Her footfalls became that of a monster stalking towards an unsuspecting prey. She was ready to fill the minds of those beyond with dreams to haunt them with unease and fear even after the sun rose and on into the day beyond, to devour their sense of safety and gladness with the returning nightmares that no amount of thrashing or screaming could make go away— all this to hush the whisper of tenderness which mistakenly left her lips.

She would forget this Mercutio. She would forget this moment of weakness. She would retreat into the world of her own comfort, glad that none were safe from her. None were exempt. She saw all and knew all, and a peaceful night's slumber was hers alone to give out as she saw fit.

But still, she paused, her heart betraying her with the strange feeling felt only once before.

"Oh liar heart," she whispered. "Harden now for me. Such bewitchment turns to affections unnatural. Remember the lessons taught to thee. Faunus, cruel teacher, schooled thee well. The devastation love brings is a price not worth the prize. Quiet. Still. Trouble me not with this siren's call. The delights thou dost tempt with shall prove bitter in taste, and thy cries of woe when all turns sour is the pain of Faunus's lesson laid to waste."

She continued on, determined not to forget. Stifling mistake's repeat would protect her from regret.

Chapter Twelve

It was mid-morning as Mercutio entered the tavern, swagger and gladness in his step. The thickly plastered walls and tiled floors of red kept the air cool and pleasant. The establishment was empty but for Romeo, whose own thoughts seemed to be a thousand leagues away.

Mercutio straddled the bench beside him and clapped him heartily upon the back. "How fares my friend? Did the fair Rosaline give you reward for your pains last night, or did her attentions only stiffen the pains that a man must endure?"

Romeo stared into his empty cup. "Ah Mercutio, endurance of such sweet agony is a worthy tithe for a moment in her love."

"Well, when it does finally flower, let us hope your long endurance does not quit upon that moment."

"A moment will be enough."

"Woe to any man who holds such sentiments hold true," Mercutio laughed as he called to the server, a short man with a bushy head of brown curls, motioning for drinks for both he and his friend.

"And what of you, Mercutio? You look no worse the wear for the celebrations of last evening," said Romeo.

Mercutio took the glasses of warmed wine from the server's ready tray and handed one to his friend. "Indeed, I slept most sound."

"Exhaustion from gentle sport?"

"Nay, my solitary bed was filled with dreams so sweet, mortal company would have been an unwelcome interloper to such unwedded bliss."

"Dreams of a particular maid?" asked Romeo.

"Bah! Maids are best for milking and I desire not their fumbling fingers. Nay, I dreamt of a stranger, a gentle lady I know not, but would fall asleep this instant if I thought I could conjure her once again," said Mercutio with a smile.

"It was a night for dreaming," Romeo stated as the server slowly cleared away the dirty dishes from the end of their empty table. "I myself dreamt of Rosaline with illusions so strong I woke having to remind myself that they were not real."

"They were probably as real as any affections you can hope to receive from the likes of her."

"Such callousness! Have you never loved, Mercutio?"

"Aye, deeply and longingly, and neither shall be had with Rosaline. Good friend Romeo, do not cast your eyes about like a fisherman's net, declaring a mackerel the finest specimen you have ever seen only because it happened to get tangled as you passed."

"So says the man with an empty net."

"Believe me, I shall not starve."

"A man without meat upon his lips withers and fades away."

"Meat not to my liking shall make me wither, too."

"Do not speak ill of my love for Rosaline," Romeo pleaded.

"You are right," Mercutio replied, gripping Romeo's forearm bracingly. "You must learn these things for yourself. My warning should be taken as no more than the ramblings of a bitter soldier who has loved and lost too much. A man whose mind wanders to a woman in his dreams and finds her more desirable than any he has seen in the flesh, perhaps because he knows for once that he shall not have to watch her die."

The silence spread as Mercutio's words hung in the air. Romeo took a long drink from his cup before speaking. "Strange, the dreams of last night."

"Aye," Mercutio said. "Believe it, my friend, despite the cloud of gloom I wear, that I woke finding the sun shining a little brighter and the woes of the world light. There was a comfort in these visions which lingers even into the day. Perhaps it is just the return home which chased away the demons that haunt me, but I have not had such restful sleep since long before the war."

"There is no bed as sweet as a man's own."

"Most days I would answer that you have not been in the beds I have known, but this morning I am wont to agree."

"Perhaps it was the faeries, sorrowful that the prince's feast came to an end, and they swept through all Verona to continue the dance where merry feet and conversation could not tire in already sleeping heads," Romeo ribbed.

Mercutio laughed as he held up his glass. "If that be the case, I shall tell my uncle we must levy a tax to play host to such welcome guests until the coffers of man have run dry."

Romeo raised his wine in fraternal agreement.

As their conversation continued on, Faunus quietly slipped into the back of the tavern and placed the tray of dirty dishes upon an empty shelf. He let his disguise fade into his true form as he mused, "These dreams bear your touch, Queen Mab. Is love the game you play? Broken hearts to break a House's back? I thought you and I exhausted this strategy before. No matter. Your first move upon the board is made, your fingers lifted from the piece. I know well how to make the counter and to send you running from your sly attack to open defeat."

Chapter Thirteen

Mab had not meant to come back the next night. Indeed, the dream which she had placed upon Mercutio would last until the full moon rode again across the night sky. Still, she reflected as she stood at the door of the prince's home, she was drawn here. There was something which caused her to come, something that guided her feet like the cool breeze leads the traveler to the mouth of a cave.

Mercutio slept within his canopied bed as if nothing had altered from the night before, except for the peace upon his face and a bowl of milk and honey which sat upon his table, as if to make his evening guest feel more at home.

She dipped her finger in the bowl, tasting the sweet richness as she gazed upon him. Her thoughts turned to the House of Montague, of how she must use this man, this beautiful human, to cause its fall. She remembered the cloak of coldness she should wrap herself in, but the taste upon her tongue, the sight of him upon her eyes, such thoughts were chased away.

Perhaps she could spare one more night, she thought, perhaps she could fool herself into believing that her curiosity was to know how best to wield her champion.

But she knew that this visit was, in fact, for something much deeper, for something which caused her deaf heart to ache.

She sat down beside him, her gown rustling like blades of grass in the wind. She passed her hand over his eyes as he inhaled the wisps of her thoughts. She followed to see what form they would take, to see when her essence mixed with his, what dreams he wished and wanted.

"You returned," Mercutio said. He was sprawled upon the ground with the ease of a school boy gazing at the sky. He looked refreshed, the wounds of heart and soul gone, his face no longer screwed in the worry of the dreams before. He held out his hand, as if waiting for Mab this whole time.

Mab looked around the dreamscape. It had not changed from the night before, not one leaf, not one star. Strange that a dreamer... this dreamer... would hold so tight to the world she had drawn.

"It is all the same," she replied, motioning around them. "You could have anything you wished."

He smiled. "It was made by you, and so I wished it to remain."

Mab gave him her hand and slowly sank down beside him. He took her arm and draped it across his stomach, the pulse of her wrist beating against the rise and fall of his breath.

"Tell me what you desire," she asked. "Riches? Wealth? Power? I can give it all to you and more."

He reached up as he replied, pausing to tenderly brush back a lock of her golden hair. "Just you."

With a wave of her hand, the night sky faded to pink and the sun rose. The sea of grass was replaced by the green of the ocean crashing upon a summer beach. A castle sat upon a hill. A white charger stood close, hooves dancing upon the sand. She waved her hand again and the sky became bright blue. A merry stream danced upon singing rocks as nude dryads giggled and chased each other upon its banks. They looked at Mercutio and called for him to join their fun. Mab once more waved and the sky was bright orange and red as the sun began to set. A throng of villagers appeared, applauding and clapping and singing songs of love for their lord. They bore tables groaning with a feast and the air was filled with the smell of wine and suckling pig.

Mercutio shook his head, turning away from the riches she offered, and whispered once again, "Only you."

She returned the world to midnight, to the quiet of just them in the field with nothing but the sister moon to keep them company.

"I am not for the keeping," she replied.

"Ah," Mercutio laughed, "Do you think I desire to clip thy wings? Nay. Better to soar like a hawk and come down to the falconer when in need of meat or drink than to be kept in a cage like a pretty songbird who is all color and no spirit."

She ran her hand along the collar of his doublet. "I do not know how to give you what you seek."

"Give me your name," was all he replied.

The words caught in her throat. A name in the mouth of an enemy could bind her, entrance her, spell her as Faunus once used it to spell her.

Mercutio took her chin in his fingertips and guided her down to his lips. "Please."

She looked into those eyes that matched the stormy sea. They held mirth, but no guile. He was a lion, content and fed, with no need to rip out the throats of those that crossed his path. Instead, he asked her to trust him with her name.

"Queen Mab," she breathed before lowering herself to press her mouth fast to his, to silence anymore questions with the act that answered them all.

In an instant, she was once more in his room. Once more he slept. And once more, she knew she should leave.

"Perhaps one more night," she whispered before flying off to fill the heads of the other dreamers of Verona, knowing that their dreams would pale next to the silent quiet she found in the arms of this, her Mercutio.

Chapter Fourteen

Faunus sat upon a rock beneath the bower of an olive tree. It jutted like a broken tooth from the top of the hill. This was his throne of nature, the seat of his power. From here he looked upon his domain of rolling hills and fertile vineyards. From here the nymphs and satyrs played.

A young man stepped forward. Faunus continued to play his pipes as he watched this boy, a lad of fine leg and just old enough to join the season, spread out the foods of pleasure: the ripe grapes plump with the early season's drought, honeyed figs, and wine.

Faunus felt his mouth hunger for these fine offerings. He rose and walked to the feast that had been laid out just for him, plucked the plumpest of fruit and allowed the juice to burst over his tongue.

The boy wore the colors of Capulet in both attire and face. Such a foolish soul to come and seek him out, reflected Faunus as he regarded him. Still, in this game that he and Mab played, this willing and desperate child might be a useful tool for unraveling the thread of Mab's existence.

The boy interrupted Faunus's thoughts. "I am Tybalt," he stated with pride.

"You are," replied Faunus. "You shall have no argument from me. Is telling me your name the reason you brought me these delights?"

"Do you enjoy my gift?" asked Tybalt.

"Indeed," replied Faunus. "Most do not remember the old gods, they seem so wrapped up with the new."

"He does not show himself to us like the gods who were here before."

"Then you have chosen wisely to bring

such offerings to my feet, for I am glad to show you my face. I shall listen to your petition for as long as your gifts bring me pleasure."

"I wish to be a great leader," Tybalt stated. "I wish to rule with justice and strength and to bring glory to the House of Capulet."

"You shall bring very little if you continue upon the road that the fates have decided."

"What?" asked Tybalt, taken aback.

"Your life shall be quite short, for in this goblet of wine that you have brought me," said Faunus, peering into the cup before taking a drink. "I see that you shall be cut down by a sword in a petty street brawl, your potential cut short, your house destroyed, all because of a Montague who feigns friendship with the House of Capulet."

"This cannot be," he cried.

"But it is and shall be, unless you become a better swordsman than a boy named Romeo. For should the House of Capulet join with the House of Montague, both shall fall. Prevent it. Nip it in the bud and you shall have your dreams. But when the foot of a Montague crosses the threshold of the Capulet's House, so shall the wheels of change be set in motion that none shall be able to halt." Faunus looked at Tybalt's stricken face. "Take heart! The words I gave you were meant to encourage, not depress." Faunus wiped his hands upon his wooly thighs. "I have eaten and I have drunk, and now I hope you may go forth to be merry. Farewell, human!"

And as Tybalt watched him disappear into the woods, the demigod's words seared themselves like a hot brand upon his mind.

Indeed, he thought, he would devote himself to be the greatest swordsman in Verona so that no man would be his match. And never would his heart be moved for those named not Capulet.

ᏚᎯᏟᎡ

Faunus paused in a glen, turning to see what Tybalt would do. He watched through the leaves of the trees as Tybalt gathered up his empty vessels like a child putting away his toys.

"What human was this?" asked a woman.

Faunus turned to find Juno standing there. Unexpected, he bowed before her and stammered out his response. "One who dreams of upsetting the delicate balance of the politics of Verona."

"And what did you tell him?"

"The truth," said Faunus. "That men like him live and die by the sword, and if he hopes to live, he had better choose to be a man."

Juno glanced at the boy who now ran through the fields, as if he could not waste a moment to follow Faunus's advice. "Strange for you to take such an interest in the House of Capulet. Tell me, Faunus, what do you seek?"

"Peace and harmony to reign upon the land."

"Liar."

"It is my duty to temper or feed the dreams of day, to adjust their reality so that by the longing or excess of it, the dreamer seeks out more. I relish my duties and do not wish for them to come to an end, but..." Faunus dragged out. "...I have learned of one who seeks too much."

Juno looked at him sharply. "Who?"

"It is as I tried to warn you. Queen Mab conspires to pull down the House of Montague."

"This complaint once more?" Juno dismissed.

"I have met her in the streets and heard of her plans. Mab's cruelty is great and her heart that of stone."

Juno stood looking up at the bright, blue sky, as if its existence could chase away the threat of eternal stars. "Take down the House of Montague, you say?"

Faunus nodded to where he had left the boy. "That child, Tybalt, is of the House of Capulet, but even I can see that if he dies, so goes the Montagues. And yet, he comes and seeks out me instead of turning to his patron. Why? For him to meet his end would accomplish the same end that Mab has long desired. It is a strange thing, Juno, and yet true. She seeks too much. Heed my words. You would not listen to me before, but listen to me now. You must banish her, take away her power over the night."

"And who would plant the seeds of dreams in the sleeping heads of all Verona?"

Faunus pulled out his pan pipes and regarded their form. Offhandedly he mentioned, "I could rule both night and day."

Juno laughed.

Faunus spoke with deadly seriousness. "She has been too long a queen and a cruel ruler to those who fall within her domain. Look at the boy as he walks back to the House of Capulet and know my words are true."

Instead Juno regarded Faunus with passive judgment, weighing his heart. "Perhaps you are correct. Perhaps the dreams of those at night and those of day should not be split longer." She nodded her head as the decision was made. "Very well. If the House of Montague should fall, Faunus, I shall give you her powers all."

Faunus smiled. He would ensure it would.

Chapter Fifteen

Mercutio was waiting for her the third night, standing on their knoll. She entered his dreams like a thief, causing the colors to shift and the light to sway. As she appeared, at once not there and then there, watching him before he turned.

"Queen Mab," he said, tasting her name like melting chocolate on the tongue, then holding out his arms to welcome her in. She rested against his strength, listening to his heart mark out the minutes and moments they had together.

"Mab," he murmured, exhaling the word like a kiss against her hair. "Wishing and wanting makes even a single touch divine. Stay with me. Do not disappear tonight."

She pulled away as he tried to meet his mouth upon hers, to confess the great sadness which she bore. "Ah, my gentle Mercutio, I cannot bring my lips to lie. If I had the power to stay forever, I would never leave your side. But alas! It cannot be. So hide with me in these stolen moments with grateful abandon, for, alack! No matter what we wish, the hour shall come with its demands and wants, and with its call, I must go back."

"And what is it that draws you away from me?"

She motioned to the world that the stood within. "I am Mab."

"And what is a Mab?" he replied, stroking her cheek.

She took his hands in hers, staying their wanderings. "I am the bringer of dreams. With my touch, the minds of all Verona slumber in fear or ecstasy. Without me, they would go mad. I birth the fantasies of the evening, bringing justice and delight to men and women no matter how poor or rich."

Such words did not cause him to recoil or repent. Instead, he kissed the fingertips entwined with his. "And what does the queen dream when she closes her eyes?" he asked.

Mab paused, her truth laid bare. "Everything which you know as true."

She took out her want and waved it. They were in her chariot high above the city roofs. "I dream of riding a hazelnut across the Verona sky drawn by creatures too small to see." She pointed to each detail. "See? The wagon wheels made from spider legs, the canopy from grasshopper wings. In my dresses made from cobwebs, I visit the homes of sleepers. And in these nightly rides, I meet people such as you."

Mercutio laughed with joy, soaring with the sensation of flight. "We float like a thistle caught up in the wind!" Mercutio looked at her in wonder. "I thought you but a dream, and never knew you to walk the world."

She showed him her home. "This is my palace. It lives outside of town. It is where I spend my nights and invisible days, a place that even you could find me now that you know my name."

"Then why do you not appear? Why do you not come during my waking hours to share the passing hours?"

"Because, my dear, your Verona is but my dream."

It gave him pause. "If these are but your dreams, what do you see when you're awake?"

She looked at him. "Do you truly wish to see?"

"Aye, my queen."

"Of all the worlds I could show you, all the pleasures a man could want, you wish to see my prison?"

"If it is a prison, then let me share your cell. It is only the solitary confinement that makes it seem to you a hell."

She waved her rosewood wand and the lush emerald hills melted to white. The stars began to fall, replaced by the icy kisses of snow. Here lay her mirror world of Verona, her home entombed in ice. A century of neglect faded its pretty face. Its untended gardens decayed and death seemed to cling to every corner. The moonlight made the world seem almost bright as day, but day would never come. They looked upon this winter, the unending cold that she alone had to endure.

Mercutio stood behind her, wrapping her in his arms to give her his warmth. "This is your world?"

"Indeed, your world is my dream, my love, and it is here, in this land of ice and cold, that I exist. One touch of the sun wakes me and I find myself here until the sun sets in your world and I can sleep once more. It has been my curse for one hundred years." Mab reached down and picked up a ball of snow. She passed it to Mercutio, and in his warm hands, it began to melt. She then took it again, and it turned to ice. "This is my tomb."

"Why are you banished, my Mab?" he asked gently.

Mab thought back to that war, to that night that she had long forgotten, the pieces she had put together over the years, and the days and dreams that followed. "There was a man that I could not sway and in my anger, I attempted to steal the heart of one whose heart was already spoken for. I was a fool and angered the gods, and so I must stand alone in these winter woods when the rest of the world frolics in the heat of the summer sun." She pointed to her palace. "I do not know which world is the more real, but I know they are both equal in emptiness and cruelty."

"No, my queen."

"No?"

Mercutio smiled and turned her towards him. "No. You are not alone to endure winter, for I am here with you now. For the first time, my fiery temper is cooled. My soul is sleepy like a hibernating bear."

"Indeed," replied Queen Mab, "and in you I finally find the warmth that I have always sought."

"Then together," suggested Mercutio, "Let us live in a shared world of dreams. As you gave to me, I give to you the key to escape. Live in my mind and heart. Rest with me, not in this icy prison, but with me, and we shall leave behind the trappings of mortal life and discover what more the world has in store."

He took her chin in his hands and tilted her face towards his. "What do you desire?"

Mab whispered, "To dream of you."

Chapter Sixteen

Faunus waited for her outside Prince Escales's palace like cat watching a mouse a-hole. He was patient, knowing she would have to emerge before sunrise, but his muscles were tense and ready to pounce. His pipes were lifted to his lips and he played a haunting tune to pass the time. As the bell tower ran one o'clock, he paused. In the darkness, Mab emerged, looking no more than a firefly exploring the highest tower, but he knew the ways of his old friend.

Faunus began to play once more, charming her down to his side.

Her chariot rested upon the wall, and with

a step she was human-sized.

"What brings you here?" she spoke in challenge.

"Strange you should come here night after night. I stop to ensure that all is right."

"I have no need of your intercession, Faunus. Begone and pretend not to lighten this pressing darkness."

Faunus tapped his chin. "Methinks you are hiding a secret, Mab."

"You thinks wrong," she replied.

He looked up at the house. "Perhaps I should investigate... Tell me true, have you been spelled or taken by a fool's trick?"

"The only fool is standing before me, and the trick is so old it has grown rank. Speak plainly, Faunus, or trouble not my sight."

"You have changed, Mab," Faunus replied, looking strangely at her face. "You are not what you once were. Whose touch causes the great queen to bend her knees and melt her heart of stone?"

"My old enemy, do I detect something akin to jealousy in your tone?"

Faunus tutted. "I know you visit this

man, you favor him with visions and dreams. Why?"

"Has the forbidden fruit caused your mouth to hunger for the meal you once set aside? He needs these dreams, and I am happy to provide."

"This man shall die and what then?"

"Why do you care, Faunus?"

Faunus placed a lip to his finger. "Tell me, do you long to leave the night, to walk within the day and light?"

She looked deep into her enemy's eyes and spoke, "Never. Keep your light. I prefer the dark."

"The dark can sometimes be quite cold for a woman by herself."

She laughed a piercing bell. "I visit the beds of every male in Verona. I spend my nights with such beauty that if Venus herself carved me gods of marble, they would seem pale and forlorn beside these human men. Empty beds and cold lonely nights do not trouble me. But perhaps they do you, my love."

Faunus sneered, "I spend my days warm in the sun with my head resting upon the laps of dryads and nymphs. I feast with the kings and give chase to the queens."

"But not this queen," Mab reminded.

He ascended his head. "Indeed, you were never wise enough to run. Instead, you sit there in your self-righteousness, practically begging to be ripped from your roost like a loudly squawking fowl as a fox sniffs in the yard."

"And are you the fox?" she asked as she circled Faunus.

He replied by circling her in kind. "To tell you would not be fox-like."

"Then there must be far greater powers who are concerned about my ability to roost."

"Nay, sweet Mab. It is only I that hunts you, but only because you were so foolish as to leave your scent around my den. And when a fox smells an injured bird, instinct comes forth, and he cannot be held at fault for going in for the kill. I remember how your heart is so easily won."

"It is, when won with magick tricks."

"Perhaps a mortal's love is better bait when trapping a queen."

Mab hated him for dangling the question like a carrot upon a string. She replied with the coldness of winter to mask the summer in her heart, hoping to lure Faunus's interest away from Mercutio's door. "Do you think I care about the lives of such lowly creatures who fornicate and feed as easily as they create and destroy? I care not for the world of man."

"They think us gods, mistaking long life for wisdom, strange shapes as things of beauty, the gift of different sight for power. How strange they will think us when they learn of our true nature," he laughed. "What foolish men these mortals be." Faunus rose from his spot and stepped closer. Queen Mab felt his power rolling off him in waves. "Stay away from this one, Mab. You know not what fates you tempt by causing him to grow once more brave and strong."

His warning gave her pause.

She asked, "Do my attentions tempt the fall of Montague? You would not feign such interest unless this man be the keystone which will cause your world to come tumbling down."

"This man is a friend of the House of Montague and I say leave him be."

"He is Prince Escales's kinsman and friend to all alike."

But Faunus smiled, seeing that his shot had struck true. No longer dismissive, Mab was now answering his warnings with arguments of logic and law. "You who know not the pleasures of earthly love and friendship do not see that there can be ties which bind a heart much stronger than the human bonds of blood."

Queen Mab raised her chin defiantly. "Think you that I do not understand the human heart?"

"Most assuredly."

"Then I shall turn his eye to Capulet. They shall welcome him to hearth and home, giving him forever an open door to their kindness."

"I know the relentless tumult of the machinations of man. I shall place blinders upon his eyes so that he shall seek no other friendship but that Montague. He shall spurn the outstretched hand of any Capulet."

"You play a poor game, Faunus, telling me of your next move. It shall be your undoing."

"Do not think your fearsome looks frighten me," he laughed. "You may be as ugly as the day is born, but do not think that you can set me trembling with your anger and your fits."

"Must you fall back on insults?" Mab asked.

"Merely the truth."

She looked at him strangely. "I appear as I have always for thousands of years. Do not think your attacks upon my vanity cut more than a blade of grass upon a dull stone."

"Then you were born foul and will die foul," he looked at her. "Though I say your appearance has grown markedly better, though still as foul as the air in a dung heap."

"I shall be sure to grow wooly legs and a horn to please you, Faunus."

"It would not harm your cause."

"You once thought me the fairest face in all of Christendom," Mab pointed out.

"Those were the days far before Christendom and it is clear that you have felt each passing year."

Mab shook her head. "Faunus, if you wish

to raise my ire, the hollow words of a foolish goat are far below the task."

"Then I would point out it is not some foolish goat but an immortal beloved who stands before you, one whom you loved, horns and all."

"Nay, Faunus, I loved only the one horn of yours at the time."

"But now I have three to please you, although it would take triple the toil to raise your favorite point."

Mab yawned. "Begone. The night is waning fast and my solitary bed awaits."

"You need only beg, and I might deign to warm it for you."

"You have your duties before you, Faunus, and I am not one."

He shrugged. "Then suit yourself. But mark my words, you might be in need of friends if you do not change your ways, Queen Mab."

She fixed him with an icy stare. "I have eaten of the fruits of your friendship long ago, friend Faunus, and found them rotten and foul."

"A beggar will find the blackest fruit delicious when the pangs of hunger strike."

"I will never be that hungry, Faunus."

Faunus gave her a wink and then made for the road.

Though he made pretence of leaving, Faunus watched from the corner of his eye until Queen Mab flew away. As soon as she was gone, he trotted into the shadowy space between two houses. He peered into the darkness. "Hear you this, Juno? Why, even warned she will not stay away! She seeks to undo the love match that you so wisely orchestrated."

The alley was at once filled with spreading peacock feathers and the goddess with the terra cotta curls delicately stepped out of hiding. Her anger was painted on her face as exquisitely as any masterpiece, but she did not reply.

Faunus pressed, insisting she respond. "Need you more proof? From her own hands, you hear her plotting the Capulets against the Montagues while using a mortal man for this destruction."

Juno turned and paced the narrow cobblestone path. Finally, she turned and gave her decision. "I shall wait to see how this game plays out, Faunus, for plotting is a far stretch from action, and wisdom might yet sway her from this path. The dreams of night are powerful and I must have proof for my own preservation, else I find myself under the scrutiny of eyes who would bore a hole even in my soul. Patience, Faunus. Let us see how the pieces fall. If they fall out of favor, well... it is not the first time a queen shall be taken by a pawn."

With a swirl once more of feathers, Juno was then gone.

Faunus looked where she left and promised, "I shall make sure it is so."

Chapter Seventeen

Faunus's words troubled Mab with a disquiet she could not shake through the remaining night and even into the day when she faded to nothing. It stayed with her when she opened her eyes and found herself awake in her world of ice. Indeed, as the sun set once more and woke again in Verona, the sense of foreboding was enough to make her fear. Would life be so cruel? Could life be so unkind? After so many years alone to give her one who knew her heart and then to take him from her?

As she drove her hazelnut across the nighttime sky and the silent sleepers below, she knew that even if it meant losing her world to Faunus, she could not allow Mercutio to be her champion. She would keep him far from these games of the gods. She would hide him from the fates and let him live as if never knowing her touch.

But she thought back to his nightmares of stone and horror. She knew this would be where his dreams would live without her there to shift their forms. Could she abandon her love? Was it any less cruel to leave him unarmed to fend against the darkness of his mind? She did not know the difference between selfish want and selfless longings anymore. She did not know how to give him the happiest days when choosing between two such terrible paths.

She rested her chariot on Mercutio's windowsill knowing that the choice would soon no longer be hers to give. And so, bravely, she stepped into his room knowing she must say goodbye.

She rested beneath the bower of the tree, a weeping willow which kissed the earth. And there drew Mercutio. He wiped the heat of the day from his brow and stepped into the blessed cool of the shadows. He knelt at her feet, throwing himself upon the spongy ground.

"You vanquished the night, my Mab. Look upon this glorious sun!" he laughed. "Upon this summer's day, I am so warm."

"And by these shadows that I live within, I am so cold," she replied.

"Cold from the heat?" he said reaching for her, "My love, let me warm you through and through."

A flock of ravens crossed the sky.

"No arms can chase away this chill," she replied, knowing what she must do, all the while praying for some sort of heavenly intercession to prevent her from doing it.

"But what of the arms of he who is more than man? Who has tasted the fruits of the other realms and sipped from the nectar of the gods? What of he who is man but is more so, too? Does he perhaps hold the heat to warm you?" He wrapped himself around her now, his heart beating in fast rhythm against her skill.

The taste of life, of human life, was intoxicating, of resting here with another instead of trapped alone.

No, she thought. She must leave this one to bear out his days in joy without her, and in doing so, save him. She gently rested her hand upon his eyes, no longer willing to tempt this fate. This battle had gone on too long. She would choose another champion and give this one the only gift she had—the gift of her protection.

And perhaps a single dream to stay with him and comfort him in the years to come.

As he closed his eyes, she whispered one word: "Forget."

Chapter Eighteen

Queen Mab looked over her shoulder at Prince Escales's palace as she flew on her nightly ride. It had been many months since the parting and, though her mind knew that it was the rightful course of action, her heart wished that it was untrue. Mercutio lived in safety there and would until the end of his days. She continued on into eternity without him, but still... her glance always fell upon the prince's palace whenever she passed by and that high tower where the keeper of her soul slept. His warmth, his laughter, his purpose, and his divine self... She had been drawn to him like a moth to flame, unaware that she was dangerously close to setting her wings on fire. Indeed, they might already have been ablaze.

She turned her chariot towards her home, the evening's dreams planted throughout Verona with a gentler touch than she normally was wont to do. A few more dreams of love's embrace, a few more visions of reunion and joy. She let her memories of Mercutio take hold in other minds, so that when she went to visit there, she would find the essence of him. Perhaps it would make her exile more bearable. Perhaps it would make the exile of mortality easier for the humans to bear, too.

She was surprised when she returned that though the hour was two o'clock, waiting outside her front door was a grand carriage drawn by a sleek matched pair of Neapolitan horses from southern Italy.

Mab rode her hazelnut to her bedchambers. Surely, something must have occurred to bring a visitor at such a late hour and with the game afoot, most likely Faunus was to blame. Only those who sought her out by name could find their way to her palace in the hidden Verona countryside. Her mind went first to trouble in the House of Capulet. Her shadow servants greeted her, tidied her hair and brushed her clothes, keeping pace with her even as she strode towards her audience hall.

The door opened before her, and standing in wait was a young man of style and foppish grace. His dark hair was slicked back against his head, his dark green tunic tailored to the height of the latest courtly fashion. At his side was a silver rapier, etched and engraved to hide the sharpness of the blade. He stretched out his leg and bowed deeply before her.

"Queen Mab," he said. "It is a pleasure."

"We have not had the pleasure of being acquainted," said Queen Mab, though she recognized him.

"I am Tybalt, nephew of Lord Capulet."

"I know," she replied.

Tybalt seemed taken aback for just a moment before recovering. "Upon my becoming a man, my uncle told me of you and the debt that you owe our House."

She bit her tongue and made her way to her throne. Sitting down, she smiled tightly. "The House of Capulet is always welcome here. To what do I owe the honor?"

He threw back his cape and advanced towards her. "My uncle told me that you swore us protection, and it is that protection that I come to speak to you about this evening."

She thought of Faunus and wondered if perhaps this Tybalt might be her champion. "It is strange your timing in coming to seek me out. Indeed, I was just thinking that I should see what bonds of friendship I might strengthen in service to your House's...loyalty."

"Half a year ago, I was told my House would fall. I seek you out to find out if I have sidestepped this fate, if I am finally safe, or if a pointed end is still written in the stars."

Queen Mab rose and walked over to her basin, her skirts swishing softly upon the floor. The basin's innards were polished to a high sheen, showing none of the wear of centuries of abuse. Each spell cast, each misspoken word, wore the rock like a thousand feet climbing the stairs of a castle. She poured the water into the tub, watching as it slowly rose to the lip, forming a perfect mirror of reflective surface which shifted with a breath. She stroked her hand three times across the surface and watched as it came to a stop. There she saw a tomb. There she saw the daughter, Juliet, plunge a dagger into her heart.

"What do you see?" asked Tybalt.

"The danger has not passed. It is just as I foretold almost a decade and a half ago to your uncle." The wager with Faunus caused the words to stick bitterly in her throat. "The end of the House of Capulet draws near."

The young man grew pale. "It is just as I feared and just as that fortuneteller predicted. He told me of my premature death. He told me to become the best swordsman in Verona, and in doing so, this cup might pass me by. This I have done! Why are we not yet safe?"

Mab leaned forward. "I see nothing of your death, only your House's fall."

"As the only male heir in the House

of Capulet, they are one and the same, are they not?"

"This fortuneteller, did he say by whose hand your death would come?"

"By a Montague! And so I have trained to best any of them in a fight, honed my sword so that I am unmatched."

Queen Mab looked once more into her basin. "Your passing is shrouded from me. If this fortuneteller told you true, keep your rapier always ready and sharp. If your death shall begin the domino's fall, far better to stay the hand which pushes it than to try and right the piece. Strike the Montague first before he can deal you a blow."

"That I gladly shall," Tybalt replied. "But if you see not my death, what harm do you predict will bring about our destruction?"

Mab turned and walked slowly back to her throne. "That which I told your uncle. As long as Juliet marries not a Montague, the House shall be safe, but fate has not yet been diverted from that path."

"Wed to someone other than a Montague?" Tybalt laughed. "Why didn't the fortuneteller say that this was all that was needed? A marriage is simple enough to arrange and something easily within my uncle's power."

"Has he found her yet a suitor?"

Tybalt thought, "Nay, she is still young. But there are many suitable enough and fitting to our family. One who would seem a blessing, not a curse, is a man named Paris..."

"I shall see to Paris," she said, cutting him off. "I will plant the seeds of desire to fit him to your cause. In doing so, I have aided your family. Go then secure in your safety."

Tybalt would not take her dismissal, demanding that she hear him through. "It is good enough to save our House, but what of tomorrow and the years beyond? How long will we delay the inevitable fall with a foe like the Montagues haranguing us at every turn?"

She sat back, lost in the possibilities of what might be.

What if she could use the downfall of the House of Montague to get that which her heart truly desired? True, this was a game to end the strife between she and Faunus. But what if it could be so much more? Mab leaned forward, seeing the opportunity to strike. "What price would you pay if I brought down the Montagues?"

Tybalt seemed to have lost his voice, unable to comprehend her words. Finally, he replied, "Anything! Any price!"

Mab looked upon Tybalt. Oh, if man only knew his power; that his words caused even the gods to seethe with jealousy. These humans could bend the heavens and override even the will of Jupiter. With a simple binding, Tybalt could grant her deepest wish. With a careful bargain, a promise to this man to see to the end a wager she had already made, this Capulet could cancel out the curse and cease her disappearance in the sunlight. Then she could spend her days at the side of Mercutio until he passed into the arms of the only lover more true than she. She couched her words carefully, so that Tybalt would not demand more in the bargain. "Nothing that will cost you anything, but something that will aid me in this task."

"Your price, Queen Mab," he demanded with an impatient tone.

She would have liked to have raked him across the face for his insolence, but once more held her tongue long enough to speak her wish. "A welcome to visit during the hours of day."

Tybalt looked at her in astonishment and then began to roar with amusement. "A welcome during the day? Why, a simple calling card will do you just as well. Truly, if you prevent tragedy from befalling my House and transfer tragedy to the door of my enemy, you can ask much more than a visit."

"Nevertheless, it is what I desire. Give me the power to visit during the day."

He shook his head. "For being a woman with the powers you claim, you are terrible at driving a bargain. My uncle could give you gold—riches beyond your wildest dreams."

"I doubt beyond my dreams," she replied.

"Indeed, beyond yours, old witch."

She stiffened. "I shall not be called an old witch."

"A woman of your years able to wield such powers of sight? Very well, do you prefer ancient sorceress? Wizened magician?

Grandmother crone?"

She looked in the mirror at her golden hair and smooth skin, puzzled at his choice of words.

He did not seem to notice and continued, "I shall call you whatever you like, but I shall not call you a wise business woman."

"All I wish is to be able to..."

"Yes, yes... Bring down the House of Montague and come during the night! Come during the day! Come any time you please! You drive a hard bargain, but I will agree to your price!" he laughed.

For the first time in centuries, Mab experienced a forgotten emotion which she vaguely remembered being called hope.

Chapter Nineteen

Paris lay upon his pillow like an angel sleeping so quietly and sweet. Surrounded by riches and wealth, his room was well appointed in iron work, velvet, and art. His face bore the marks of Capulet, black hair slicked straight and olive skin. Perhaps he could be her champion, Mab thought. At night, Paris was a different story to the terror he inspired in the courts at day. Before this moment, she particularly delighted in leaving him with nightmares, knowing they were the price required to absolve his daily sins. One did not live a life of cruelty without reaping the rewards.

She regarded him with disdain. He could take the taste of kindness and she would not feel ill at ease for using him as her pawn. She even wondered what he would be like to have a conscience to tend his soul. But the die was not yet cast in this game, and she was not sure if this was the piece she wished to play. For tonight, she would fulfill the promise to Tybalt to sway this Paris to woo, and nothing more.

"Paris," she whispered.

He sighed as he turned onto his side.

"I must tell you of your happy destiny, of a future so bright that one such as you is undeserving."

She paused for a moment, a strange sense of regret weighing upon her for brokering the harsh marriage of Lord Capulet's daughter, Juliet, to this boy. She tried to comfort herself in the knowledge that happiness was but a fleeting thing, a momentary lie to make the world bearable. It was something to dream about and hope for, but a place never to live. Mab knew the girl would survive well enough, as all women had endured since time immortal. Mab had promised the Capulets protection, and this marriage would ensure that the House's precious daughter would not die.

Still, there was something about it which gave her pause.

She thought of how easy the hours were when spent in the company of love. She would be condemning this girl to her own frozen prison to marry her to this man. She looked once more at Paris, wondering kind of jailor he would be.

But if she let Juliet die, the Capulet House would fall. Faunus would win and Mab would be condemned forever. The decision seemed clear, and yet, she had to force herself to say, "Tomorrow, County Paris, you are to go to Lord Capulet and make your suit. You will keep the bloodline strong, benefiting you and countless others. Make Juliet your wife before some young man's pretty face sways her good sense and another suitor preys upon her loyalty and virtue. Seek suit from her father and protect the House of Capulet."

Paris nodded in his sleep and a cruel smile

fell across his face.

She paused for a moment, wondering if the cruelty was any greater than her own.

Chapter Twenty

Mab was careful to stand in the shadows of the dining room, the mid-morning light shuttered and dim to keep out the heat of the day, and listened quietly as Lord Capulet and County Paris talked—one man she had sworn to protect, and one who might be able to stave the fall of the first's House. She needed to see if the dreams she planted were quick, or whether they required further tending before the thoughts could be harvested in the sun.

Lord Capulet had not changed so much from when she saw him those fifteen years ago. His face was lined, and those emotional etchings spoke of the harshness of his ways since. Indeed, he was angered this morning due to a chaotic scene his men had wrought in the town square, a meaningless brawl which had brought the ire of Prince Escales down upon his head.

"That nephew Tybalt of mine stirred up trouble once again with his strutting and preening. But at least the Montagues cannot strike back," Lord Capulet assured Paris, "For we are both bound by the prince's decree to keep peace in the streets. It is not hard for old men like me, but who is to say what hot-headed young men are capable of?" He gave Paris a knowing wink. "And who is fool enough to think that they might listen to their elders? Especially if their elders are slow to speak."

Paris coughed and shifted impatiently. "Slow to speak seems wise in this situation with the prince, but to our business, Lord Capulet, speedily spoken words would seem the more desirable course. What say you to my suit? What thinks you of my proposal to bind your house to mine through the bonds of marriage between myself and your daughter, Juliet? The wisdom of this match came to me as if in a dream. From every angle I can see it is a profitable venture."

Lord Capulet chewed thoughtfully upon the grape and spat the seeds out upon his plate. "She is too young."

"Younger than she are happy mothers made."

Lord Capulet shook his finger at Paris. "And too many her age taken too soon. She is my only child, Paris, and the only hope I have to carry on my line." Lord Capulet rose and walked to the window. He clasped his hands behind his back, silent as he thought. He turned his head over his shoulder and said, "Still, I hear your words and I will not deny there is wisdom in it. I tell you this: Get her heart, Paris. I might give my consent, but it is hers which tells me where to give it. Tonight, I hold a feast. I have invited all the best families of Verona, all those that I hold dear. Come. Look upon the ladies as they emerge from winter's grasp. Their dowries and inheritances are as large as my Juliet's. If you gaze upon all these maidens and still are wont to woo my daughter, and my daughter deigns to look upon you, you shall have my blessing."

Lord Capulet waved to his servant to follow him as he went to his desk. He picked up his quill and, inking it, placed it up on the parchment to write out his wishes. "Go, servant, and trudge through fair Verona to find those persons whose names are written here. Welcome them all to a masque at the home of Lord Capulet tonight." Lord Capulet turned to Paris. "We shall see what temptations I can lay before you and will not think you less a man if you manage not to escape from their grasp."

Lord Capulet finished the list, blowing upon the ink to quicken setting. He rolled the paper and handed it over to his servant, who bowed and left to invite the guests.

Queen Mab nodded, pleased Paris had listened so wisely to her council. The game had now begun and was stepping smartly to the tune she played.

Chapter Twenty-One

Faunus sat in the marketplace, delighting in the wanderings of the humans about him. These mortals fought and haggled for desires which would scarcely survive the week. He fed them spirit to keep their ire sharpened, caring not about the effects of the chaos. He, himself, fed upon the bitter strife for the things that would be forgotten by day's end. But it was not for these joys that he was drawn today to the busy sellers' square.

He did not have to wait long, for soon entered a dark blonde man, a hulking brute of brawn. This man made for his kinsman, Romeo, who was sat reclined upon the steps of a wine merchant, the effects of such wares already coloring Romeo's day. Faunus listened in like a spy, waiting the words which might be wielded as weapons against these children of Montague, these offspring of that House which Juno, for some reason, held so dear. Faunus had other plans and was happy to play his part in fate.

"Good morning, cousin," greeted Benvolio.

"Is the day so young?" replied Romeo. His face held the shadows of unrequited love, his heart troubled and aching with yearning. Faunus understood the aching loins of youth and found it strange this young man would stay in misery and not seek out some satisfaction.

"What sadness lengthens your hours?" asked Benvolio.

"Want for the one thing that makes the hours fly," said Romeo, taking another drink from his half-empty skin of wine.

"In love?"

"Out--"

"Of love?" asked Benvolio.

"Out of her favor," sighed Romeo.

With half an ear, Faunus listened to Romeo swear love for a wench called Rosaline, bemoaning the chaste future she had vowed to live.

Faunus looked down upon this Montague, his straw colored curls peeking out from beneath his cap. Faunus thought aloud to himself, "This gives me ideas a plenty. Why, who is this Rosaline? Not one who could cause the House of Montague to fall. But perhaps one far fairer than she... How much more appalling that a man such as Romeo should love and be spurned by Capulet's daughter? Who knows what havoc it might play? Only the gods themselves... and I. That is how I shall bring his ruin. Such a simple thread to pull, to unravel his story before it does begin!" He clapped his hands with glee. "Ah, Mab, someday you shall see that we both were playing the same side of the board, but I alone shall win!"

Faunus looked on in interest as a courtly messenger wandered lost through the streets. He slipped behind him and glanced over the man's shoulder. He seemed to bear a list of names. Spying the name of Rosaline, Faunus cloaked himself in the illusion of a musician and placed his hand upon the servant's shoulder. "Pray, gentle sir, you look to be lost."

The messenger practically leapt in surprise. "Forgive me! I did not see you there! Indeed, I am looking for many a noble face and foot to attend a masque at the home of Capulet."

"Ladies and gentlemen giving chase to worldly delights in the court of Capulet! What joyful sport! Are you having trouble finding the joiners of your feast?"

The servant nodded. "My master bade me to invite these that are listed here, but alas, I cannot read. Can you, sir?"

Faunus shrunk back. "Oh no, not I! I am but a poor musician who plays his pipes to bring joy to people's day. But I saw those two men there looking upon a note." He directed the servant's attention to Romeo and Benvolio. "They seem to be gentlemen of honorable means. Speak to them, and I am sure they would be glad to assist you in your quest."

"Oh thank you!" bobbed the servant. "Thank you! For you have saved me! Thank you, kind sir!"

"Speak nothing of it," Faunus replied, sending him on his way.

He watched as Romeo gladly read the messenger the names, pausing as he said both Mercutio and Rosaline.

Gratefully, the servant said to the two men, "Please join the masque! If you be not from the House of Montague, you are welcome to the house of my master, the Lord Capulet! It begins tonight at sunset, and I should be glad to see you there! Now, I bid you thanks and goodbye."

Benvolio's eyes sparkled as he took Romeo's arm. "Rosaline shall be there and so we shall go! Compare her face with some that I shall show, and I will make thee think thy swan a crow."

Romeo shook his head. "Never! I shall go to prove your eyesight wrong, and bask in the beauty of the one to whom my heart belongs."

Benvolio clapped his arm around Romeo's

shoulders and steered him to home to plan for the upcoming evening's events.

Faunus smiled, wishing he could be there to see it all, knowing that this was the genesis which would begin Mab's fall.

Chapter Twenty-Two

Mab stood in the doorway of a darkened house, the sounds of merriment echoing down the cobblestone streets of Verona as the city prepared for the night's festivities. Dusk crept over the horizon and once more she could step into this world of flesh and blood. She listened to the prattle of a coming party of revelers, masked and merry.

As they turned the corner, Mab recognized the first man in the mob—Romeo. His eye turned towards any maiden who glanced his way, the yearning of his faux melancholy wielded as seductive trick. Mab had known men like him over the centuries. She had sat hidden in the corners of many a poor girl's room as she wept, as if the tears from her eyes could carry away the darkness stifling her heart. Oh, she had known men like Romeo.

He was followed by Benvolio, a friend of all might and no matter, whose dull wit and serious ways would bore a maiden as sure as Romeo would break her heart.

But then followed another man who stole Mab's very breath away.

"Mercutio," she whispered.

The pain of parting was as fresh and new as if it had happened only yesterday. The wound she thought had been healing proved itself a liar, striking her with an arrow of regret for the moments they had not been together. She was filled with yearning to go to him, to throw herself in his arms and escape into the worlds they once built side-by-side.

"Give me a torch, I am not for this ambling," Romeo complained, reaching out to take it from Mercutio's hand.

With a twinkle in his eye, Mercutio lifting it high above his head, causing his friend to leap after it. "Nay, gentle Romeo, we must have you dance!"

"Not I, believe me. You have dancing shoes with nimble soles, I have a soul of lead which so stakes me to the ground I cannot move," he replied as he jumped.

"You are a lover, borrow Cupid's wings, and soar with them above a common bound," said Mercutio, taking off down the street.

Queen Mab lost them as Romeo gave angry chase, trying hard to catch up with Mercutio's wit. They turned the corner into an alleyway, and their voices became muffled. She sped to keep pace and watch them at their game.

Mercutio had his arm around his friend's neck, churlishly advising, "If love be rough with you, be rough with love. Prick love for pricking and you beat love down." He gave Romeo a kiss upon his crown and then turned to the revelers in his midst. "Give me a mask to cover myself in." He grabbed one from Benvolio, looking it over with delight. "Ah! An ugly mask for my most ugly face! What care I if a curious eye looks upon this mask with its deformities? Here are the beetle-shaped brows which shall blush for me and leave my face always the improvement when this veil is removed."

Romeo sat upon the step, a skulking bundle of passion, surrounding himself with the blackness of rainclouds and storms.

"I dreamt a dream tonight," said Romeo to Mercutio.

"And so did I," replied his friend, trying to rouse Romeo and steer him to the dance.

"Well, what was yours?"

"That dreamers often lie."

Romeo corrected him. "In bed asleep, while they dream things true."

Mercutio stopped, turning to Romeo. He became as pale as one who has seen a ghost. "O, then I see Queen Mab hath been with you."

Queen Mab was a hind who caught the smell of a hunter. His words were ones that should not be. She had promised him forgetting, abandoned him to the night. That he should remember her touch at all seemed to say that something was not right.

Romeo paused, giving Mercutio a puzzled look.

"She is the fairies' midwife," Mercutio explained, searching his friend's face for kindred recognition. "And she comes in shape no bigger than an agate stone on the forefinger of an alderman. Drawn with a team of little atomies over men's noses as they lie asleep."

Mab quietly pressed herself against the wall, desperately wanting to hear the memories which Mercutio held so dear he could not be forced by her, with all her power, to forget.

"Her wagon spokes made of long spinners' legs," he said, coaxing Romeo to reminisce with him. "The cover, of the wings of grasshoppers; her traces, of the smallest spider web; her collars, of the moonshine's watery beams; her whip, of cricket's bone; the lash, of film; her wagoner, a small grey-coated gnat, not half so big as a round little worm pricked from the lazy finger of a maid."

Romeo and Benvolio acted as if these words nothing more than fancy, but Mercutio went on insistent, as if he hoped somehow he could open the door to his friend's memory and Romeo would suddenly cry, "Ah yes! I know her, too!" But he was met instead by indulgent smiles.

"Her chariot is an empty hazelnut, made by the joiner squirrel or old grub, time out o' mind the fairies' coachmakers," Mercutio said, painting the picture in the air before him. "And in this state she gallops night by night through lovers' brains, and then they dream of love; over courtiers' knees, that dream on curtsies straight; over lawyers' fingers, who straight dream on fees; over ladies' lips, who straight on kisses dream."

Mercutio stepped closer to his friend, gripping his shirt desperately in the hopes of understanding. "Sometimes she gallops over a courtier's nose, and then dreams he of smelling out a suit; and sometimes comes she with a tithe-pig's tail tickling a parson's nose as he lies asleep, then dreams he of another benefice. Sometimes she driveth over a soldier's neck, and then dreams he of cutting foreign throats, of breaches, ambuscadoes, Spanish blades, of healths five fathom deep; and then anon drums in his ear, at which he starts and wakes, and being thus frighted, swears a prayer or two and sleeps again."

Frustrated that Romeo still stared upon him blankly, Mercutio tore himself away and shouted, "This is that very Mab that plats the manes of horses in the night and bakes the elflocks in foul sluttish hairs, which once untangled much misfortune bodes. This is the hag, when maids lie on their backs, that presses them and learns them first to bear, making them women of good carriage. This is she!"

Romeo interrupted, coming over to hold his friend silent and still, thinking it was the ramblings of a madman. "Peace, peace, Mercutio, peace! You talk of nothing."

Even though his friends did not know his meaning, Mab heard and knew. There was such an aching sadness of loss as Mercutio opened his mouth that Mab thought her heart might break. He seemed almost ashamed for his remembrances, for being one of the chosen few who had walked among the fair folk and had knowledge when he should not. He bowed his head, staring at his hands as though to speak the lies the world might ask, to deny the truth that he knew was true, was more than a man should shoulder.

But he said the words anyways, to bring comfort to his friends. "True, I talk of dreams, which are the children of an idle brain, begot of nothing but vain fantasy, which is as thin of substance as the air and more inconstant than the wind, who woos even now the frozen bosom of the north, and, being angered, puffs away from thence, turning his face to the dew-dropping south."

Queen Mab could not bear it. She whispered to Benvolio to hasten their steps to the Capulets, so that drink and song might cause her Mercutio to laugh once again and bring a carefree smile to this face she held so dear.

"This wind you talk of blows us from ourselves," interrupted Benvolio, tired of being distracted and pointing to the home of Capulet. "Supper is done and we shall come too late."

As they left, Mab looked up in the night sky, filled with such bittersweet happiness for this moment, savoring every word and reliving the rumble of Mercutio's voice in her bones.

But this peaceful revelry was suddenly replaced with a deep foreboding, some sense that tonight began a terrible march towards some destiny that not even she could forestall.

She looked over at the men as they made their way and heard Romeo speak. "My mind misgives some consequence yet hanging in the stars shall bitterly begin his fearful date with this night's revels and expire the term of a despised life closed in my breast by some vile forfeit of untimely death..."

His voice trailed off.

Indeed, thought Mab, even the fool Romeo felt it true.

Chapter Twenty-Three

Queen Mab stepped inside the ballroom, masked in black velvet and gold. The room was filled with costumed guests, anonymous in their masquerade. Mab looked across the room and saw Lord Capulet. He was red-faced and sweating before even the first hours of the ball had departed.

Lord Capulet turned to her, as if he felt her eyes upon him. She saw him swallow uncomfortably as he recognized her and did not understand why there should be this faerie queen, this demigod of dreams in their midst. As he left the small group he was engaged with and teetered through the crowds to her side.

He bowed graciously before her and murmured politely his greetings of joy. "My memory of you comes flooding back as if our meeting occurred only yesterday."

She smiled. "Indeed, I am sure that is quite the case. For me, each year almost seems to pass as quickly as the days."

"You are welcome here to our humble home, Queen Mab, and I extend our hospitality."

"I should hope one such as you would not have forgotten the old ways."

"No indeed, my queen," he turned to a servant and spoke in low tones. "Milk and honey for this guest."

The servant bowed deeply and skittered away.

"What brings you to our simple gathering?" Lord Capulet asked as baskets of rose petals fell from above like rain, causing his guests to laugh and clap in delight.

She could see he was trying to clear his head, trying desperately to rid himself of the swaying of the room so that he might be able to focus solely upon her.

From his glassy-eyed visage, she knew it was a losing battle.

"Fifteen years ago, I gave you a pronouncement. A very important prediction which would best be served if it was remembered," she said.

Lord Capulet looked into his glass, trying to remember what it was.

"Your daughter," reminded Queen Mab.

"What about my daughter?" asked Lord Capulet.

"How swiftly the mortal mind forgets," sighed Queen Mab. "Tonight, she meets her husband-to-be, a man in whom she might take refuge, and in doing so, build a protection for all the House of Capulet."

"And who is this man?"

"Why, the County Paris, a man of good breeding and taste who would make a fitting son to your family," she replied.

Lord Capulet clapped in delight. "You and I are of one mind and to this my heart is easily joined." Lord Capulet waved at his ballroom floor. "You are welcome here to dance and sing among my party guests and to welcome the end of that which would end this House. Drink! Be merry! Work your ways without fear of interference. I shall be your partner in this cunning intrigue."

At that moment, Romeo and his party passed. Queen Mab should have told Lord Capulet to eject them, but the sound of Mercutio's gentle ribbing and explosive laughter among these friends held her tongue. She could not send him away. Instead, she retired behind a column as Tybalt greeted the enemy at the door.

"This, by his voice, should be a Montague." Tybalt turned to his page and commanded, "Fetch me my rapier, boy."

"Why, how now, kinsman! Wherefore storm you so?" asked Lord Capulet. His attention was upon Mercutio. Lord Capulet placed his hand upon his nephew's arm, urging him to notice Prince Escales's kinsman. But Tybalt would not be silenced, each man unaware that the other was in a battle for survival.

"Uncle, this is a Montague, our foe, a villain

that is hither come in spite, to scorn at our solemnity this night," Tybalt explained.

Lord Capulet followed his glance and remarked, "Young Romeo is it?"

"Tis he, that villain Romeo."

With soothing words, Lord Capulet tried to cool his nephew's fiery temper. "Content thee. Let him alone."

Tybalt let out a snort.

Lord Capulet continued, "He has a reputation to be a virtuous and well-governed youth, proved in the company he keeps." Lord Capulet gave a meaningful glance to Mercutio. "I would not for the wealth of all the town disparage him in my house. Pay Romeo no mind."

Tybalt made a move to make argument, but Lord Capulet silenced him. "It is my will, which you will respect. Do not shame me with your frowns and inhospitable storms which do not fit the joy of this feast."

Tybalt's face became dark. "It fits when such a villain is a guest. I'll not endure him."

Lord Capulet turned and rebuked. "He shall be endured! I say he shall! Am I the master here or you? Go to. You'll not endure him! God shall mend my soul! You shall make a mutiny among my guests!"

"Why, uncle, it is a shame," Tybalt insisted.

"Be quiet!" he replied, cuffing his nephew across the ear. Tybalt stood in shock as the entire room fell quiet at the sound of the strike. Lord Capulet straightened his tunic. He looked about the room to face the reproachable silence and called out, "More light, more light! For shame! I'll make you quiet. What? Is this a celebration or no? Cheerily, my hearts!"

Tybalt watched as Lord Capulet stumbled off to yell for more music or fire, anything to bring distraction, and Tybalt quietly withdrew.

Queen Mab looked on, knowing this Tybalt was the man she would have to endure in the years to come. Still, no matter her reservations, she reminded herself, she was here to see to his ascent, no matter how distasteful it might be. To protect the House of Capulet, she must be light of foot and ready to dance with her partner, young love, whose complicated footsteps would keep her on her toes.

She edged her way around the ballroom, the flickering light of the candles settling a golden glow upon the revelers.

Lord Capulet's daughter descended from her rooms and all eyes turned to see who joined the feast. She was a delicate vision of loveliness, spun sugar which begged for gentleness so as not to break. Her thick brown hair was wound in braids to form a crown upon her head. Her gown of pink gossamer silk floated with each step, seeming to slow the world with its whispering sighs. Modest jewels upon her bodice and neck seemed to shine a light upon the true gem they could not adequately adorn. As Juliet's slippered foot left the stairs and touched the floor, Mab was pleased to see Paris there to bow low before her and lead her out into the dance. The young maiden seemed open to his overtures and willing to listen to the compliments and niceties of his lips. Lute and woodwind piles played as the two found quiet comfort in the touch of a hand and foot.

But Queen Mab's eyes were taken from this

couple and fixed like a magnet to north, for crossing hands in the intricate patterns of the Amoroso was Mercutio. His face was alight with joy and life as his feet lifted off the ground. The ladies giggled at his exuberance, but Mab felt something quite different stir within her heart. Perhaps it was jealousy, perhaps envy, but it was indeed a longing so deep that it made the mighty oceans seem like shallow rivers. He was a creature of two worlds, not just friend to these two Houses estranged, but a dancer of both light and dark, a human who had tasted both worlds and found them equally delicious. A man with terrible pain and terrible happiness. He had eaten his fill until the hunger in his soul had been sated, and now he brought both together as a whole.

She ripped herself away, knowing that to reach out to him once more would be his doom. As she stepped out of the ballroom and into the night air, the fireflies within her dress lit, bathing her in a soft, otherworldly light. The flagstones gave way to a tended garden with topiaries, fountains, and tall hedges made for hiding.

The gentle laugh of cavorting lovers stopped her in her tracks. Mab looked and saw Juliet was no longer at the side of Paris. Instead, she watched as Romeo and Juliet, palm to palm, stared into one another's eyes until their lips spoke the words that their breath could not.

Mab sent out her will, forcing Juliet's nurse to call, to stop this fate before it began. But then these two lovers' lips parted, and Mab recognized that moment of holy stillness. She had known it with Mercutio, and the span of her thousands of years told her that it was divine.

There must be another way, she thought, lifting the vial of Capulet's kindness from the chain around her neck.

She looked upon it, warm and glowing in her hand. The sound of Juliet being called once more back into the party drifted across the garden.

It suddenly seemed so foolish to waste a drop of such a gift on a mortal, Mab thought. They had enough to spare and jealously kept it close or heedlessly gave it away.

She turned to gaze upon Mercutio inside, his eyes smiling in the lamplight as he laughed at the witticisms of one who did not deserve his attention. Mab missed him, missed the lessons of his gentle, careless ways. She did not even know until now that she was and always would be his pupil, learning the sweetest lessons of the world from the dreams they shared, of the instruction she found navigating the heart.

It suddenly seemed quite strange that she would think such a wager, which would have her even consider turning such a man into her champion, was sound. Why had she staked this gift of kindness so hardly won upon a peace with Faunus? Peace with or without him was none of her desire.

No.

It was of Faunus's desire. As it always had been, ever since he tricked her from her sacred bull and stole that night of dreams from her. Always Faunus. Always his wants. Always his schemes.

She would not play his game. Clarity

ringing through her mind. Unstoppered, she lifted the vial to her lips. In a single draught, she swallowed down the sweet taste.

It was richer than the richest nectar she had ever eaten in the forest of forgetting. It warmed her as it traveled down her body, filling her with a glow within and without. She looked upon the world as if after all those centuries, she had never gazed upon it before. She looked upon the ballroom, upon the mortals dancing there, so delicate, so frail, untended and unwatched by one with power. She felt a need build up inside of her, to wrap them in her arms and tuck them off to bed. To fill their minds with the most beautiful dreams imaginable so that the drudgery of living would be easier day by day.

She watched as Romeo left the party, yearning to call him back. His face was stricken first by some words of Benvolio, and then of Lord Capulet, who soon stumbled off to bed and called the revelry to an end. As the confused party goers made their way to the door, Mab hastily followed, trying to give chase to Romeo as he headed into the darkness. The kindness she had stolen burned her with remorse. The memories of her past actions caused her to recoil like touching white hot coals. But born from these ashes was a new desire: to stop the fall of either House no matter what the cost.

Chapter Twenty-Four

Mab watched as Romeo climbed the Capulet's wall and went over with youthful joy. He made straight towards the balcony of his Juliet.

Oh that she could turn this hand and take back the wager with Faunus. Mab tried to keep her thoughts upon the path that must be, this daughter and the County Paris. She wanted to call out to Romeo to come back and she would plant the seeds of love within Rosaline. But she could not, frozen by the power of that human feeling which caused him to risk his life. Love. Oh, the love that drove him! It was beyond rapture. A drink of the divine to quench the longing thirst of the heart.

Her ears pricked as she heard the voices of those who might be able to save this boy.

Benvolio called, "Romeo! My cousin Romeo!"

Mab gave his words wings and sent them over the wall to his kinsman, but Romeo would not be stopped.

Then Mab heard the voice of Mercutio. It rang like a bell in her soul, its sound rippling its toll from toe to fingertip.

He placed his hand upon Benvolio's arm. "He is home by now and in bed."

She felt deep within her bones how cruel it was to have left Mercutio, even for his own protection. She felt how unkindly she abandoned him to face the world without that which they shared to fend off the buffeting winds. She stood immobile, wanting to fling herself into his arms and beg for his forgiveness, but knew he would not recognize her, not even know what sorrow plagued her. She herself had seen to that. All he had was a vague memory of a dream woman who flew across the sky in a hazelnut.

Even as these emotions tore within her, the world continued without care. Benvolio insisted, "He ran this way, and leaped this orchard wall. Call, good Mercutio!"

Mab reflected the wish, hoping that Mercutio would heed his words.

"Nay, he hears not, he stirs not, he moves not."

"Call!"

Mercutio laughed, leaping atop the stones that separated their path from the land of Capulet. "Romeo! I conjure thee by Rosaline's bright eyes, by her high forehead and her scarlet lip! By her fine foot, straight leg and quivering thigh, and the areas that there adjacent lie!"

Benvolio hushed his friend. "You will anger him! He has hid himself among these trees. Blind is his love and best befits the dark."

Mercutio shook his head. "If love be blind, love cannot hit the mark. Romeo, good night! I'll to my bed. This field is too cold for me to sleep. Come, shall we go?"

"Go, then," Benvolio said, waving him goodbye.

Mercutio stumbled away to find a place to rest from the evening's intrigue. A whistling tune upon his lips, he wandered carelessly up the street.

She should flee before he reached her hiding place, but the sight of him through new eyes was almost more than Mab could bear. She felt her cheeks, and there was a wetness there, as if rain had fallen, but there was no rain in the sky. She stared at her hand, unbelieving and unknowing.

"Why do you weep?" asked a voice.

She looked up and there he was, her beloved Mercutio, stepping out from the shadows to inquire about the happiness of a stranger. He was both familiar and strange. She was filled with something that she now could only describe as love. She could not speak. She could not move. Just weep for the callousness with which she was going to play these Houses, ready to ruin lives for nothing but a game.

"I know thee," he spoke in astonishment,

as the things meant never to be remembered begged once more their place within his mind. He reached out, as if to touch her, as if to brush away the tears she did not know could fall, but then stopped. He examined her face for the solution to the mystery. "I remember thee as if in a dream. From whence do I know thee? From a ball or a feast or upon a throne of gold and ebony?"

She took his hand, its calloused palm and male roughness and held it to her face. "From all those things, for we have danced and been merry and mended the wounds that time could not. I am of one world and another, but I am sworn forever to protect thee, and in protecting thee, I do love thee. Forgive me," she whispered before disappearing into the night, leaving the world to the steady march of fate.

Mercutio watched her, puzzled as she flew. But then the dreams came back, as fresh as if he had never woke. His heart pounded, his mind raced, that this woman who existed only in his mind had just stood before him in the flesh. He would not let her hide to bear these dreams alone, not since she had shown him the world. He desperately gave chase and vowed he would run to the ends of the earth and beyond to gain her heart once more.

Chapter Twenty-Five

Mab gripped the railing of her balcony and looked out upon her sprawling land. At night, it teased of the warmth and green always beyond her touch. Inside her home, it was so cold and dark, such a strange contrast to the feelings which coursed through her tonight.

Her heart had fought a war over the century to stay as cold as the inner shadows of her retreat, but now with each moment that she breathed with this taste of kindness upon her tongue - one breath was the world, another began the world anew.

Her mind was awash in the nevers and forevers she had promised herself, which now knocked gently at her door. To love a mortal... to open her heart to one who had already aged from a child to a man and soon to a wrinkled creature of skin and bone who would fade into nothing but a memory until he was forgotten. One generation, perhaps two, and all who held him in their mind would be gone and she would be left alone night after night, remembering the way his pulse pounded in his veins whenever she drew close. Nothing more.

This was the fate of love. She had seen finer, stronger faeries than she fade to mere shadows due to the intoxicating power of a mortal's affection. Even Queen Titania, mourning the loss of her changling, fell so far on a midsummer's eve as to love an ass. Such was the price of vulnerability.

Mab looked at her domain and wondered if it was worth sacrificing everything for this, her Mercutio. Her traitorous heart told her yes.

"Oh, what a man is this," she whispered, "He who can turn my thoughts and turn my head, and in doing so, turn this world upside down. Such a strange creature, made of flesh and blood which will grow old with age, which will fade and decay like the sunset. Perhaps for a moment, we will have the brilliant swaths of orange and gold and red passion painted across the sky. But always the dark creeps over the horizon. How can I love knowing that one day the morning will never come again? Illusions of real and imaginary... Are the worlds I paint not just as fine as the world I look upon? Finer still, I say!"

"But no world as fine as the ones we shared in those dreams of own making," said a voice from far below.

Mab looked down from her balcony. In the moonlight was the raven-haired man with the eyes of ocean green her heart longed for.

"How long have you been standing there?" she asked.

"Long enough to hear, long enough to remember. Each exquisite word was like a drop of water upon a man's parched tongue, a balm upon a heart that was broken by a foolish woman's unkindness."

"I never meant to be unkind," Queen Mab

whispered.

"Of all that was and ever will be in my life, I know," said Mercutio. "Indeed, you were the first taste of kindness my heart and soul knew after a long drought, coming to me when harsh words and hard hands had broken my very spirit."

Queen Mab wiped her cheek and leaned upon the stone railing. "And you I. A century I have lived with beings mortal and immortal recoiling from my sight, but you saw and did not cringe back with fear."

"How could anyone cringe from you? How could they fear you, my love?" He grabbed ahold of the trellis and slowly began to climb to her balcony. "That which caused them to recoil was the reflection of their own soul, to which you hold up a mirror, but any who did not long to give up their lives to live in your arms never saw your true face."

"And what is it you see reflected back at you?" asked Mab.

Mercutio reached the top of the trellis and leaned over the balustrade to take her hand. "The reflection I see in you is love, and the reflection I give back is the same." He laid his warm fingers upon her cheek, tracing the lines of her jaw and her lips. "I see all my dreams reflected in you. I see my happiness in your eyes. I hear my joy in your breath. And I feel peace which can only be granted with your lips."

And he bent and gently touched his to hers.

She did not disappear or awaken in another place. Instead, she stayed here with him and something inside her melted, a great glacier slowed in its ever present march as if in spring to feed the pools of life that longed to fill themselves with man's love.

They parted, a breath away.

"My heart has always belonged to you, my queen. My heart and soul and mind. I only lived when you joined me those nights. I did not know that I died when you went away. Indeed, I had been the walking dead. Laughing and jesting, but dead as if a thousand years in the ground. But with the touch of your lips, I feel as if the fountain of youth has restored me. I feel as if the door to heaven has been opened and once more my lifeless body can spring o'er the hills. This is the power of but one kiss. You are the woman I have dreamed of, without knowing it was you. And now I wake and see the dream is real, that the woman is here, that you are here, and I do not wish to sleep again."

"But you must sleep someday, my mortal love," she whispered, "And it is that eternal sleep which keeps me from your side."

"But what dreams we might have together here and now," he replied, placing his lips aside her ear and brushing them softly with each word. "Such dreams so that when I must close my eyes, they will make the heavens seem dull. I was dead without you, but now live knowing that I might look forward to basking in the warmth of your sun."

"I am not the sun," she protested, her hands trying to memorize his face so that when he was taken from her she might never forget. "I am the moon."

"Then let me be thy sun, let me warm thy days so that thou can reflect back my light with the darkness comes. Without me, thou shalt be forever in cloaked in black, gently orbiting the earth with no one to see."

"Such loneliness is my duty," she replied.

"But with me, there is one who will illuminate your path, so that those who do choose to gaze on thee can see the beauty thou art to behold." Parting, he brushed back a tendril of hair that had loosened itself.

Once more their lips met, only this time it was hers that crossed the distance as he stood steady, waiting for her to decide.

Slowly, he lifted one leg and then the other over her balcony rail until he stood beside her, his arms chasing away the chill, wrapped around her like a summer's breeze, warming her to her core.

Chapter Twenty-Six

"Mercutio..." she murmured, stirring quietly in the silken sheets of her bed.

"Mab," he replied, his lips still swollen from pressing upon hers.

She traced her fingers around his curls, feeling at once like she could disappear into nothingness or explode into creation and all the world would be right.

"What do you think of, dear Mab?" he asked. His lips formed a smile, slight and secret, and one eye drooped in pleasured exhaustion.

"How strange a name..." she murmured.

"What means you?" he laughed, his chest

rumbling the sounds like echoes in a cave against her ears.

"Mab. A small word with an 'm' and a 'b' and nothing but the sound of sorrow to keep the two apart."

"You may call yourself Gwenyvere and my love for you would not change. You are Mab, my Mab, a small name fit for a mighty queen."

"A queen of a kingdom imagined."

"A queen of my heart and that is not imagined."

"This world that we live in will fade soon, and I will wake to see that I have merely fallen asleep in another place and time."

"But for now, this is truth and for now, think not of the other worlds to be," spoke Mercutio gently, gathering her close. "Even though this is but a moment in the blink of an eye for you, it shall be something I carry with me for my lifetime. All that I remember, all that I will be or will not be, you will color it all like a wash from a painter's cup. In fact, you already do."

"As do you my love."

He stroked her hair, the peace of the early

morning upon their union.

"Promise me you will never leave while breath stirs within my lungs," asked Mercutio.

"I am afraid that is a promise I cannot keep," replied Mab.

"And why not?" he asked. "Why must you leave when together the waking is even sweeter than the dreaming?"

Her smile was sad, her heart full of longing as she looked at him and saw he did not remember the tragedy of their dream. "I must disappear with the first light of the sun. So it has been every morning for one hundred years, and will be every morning for a hundred years beyond. Sometimes I may cling to those bits of night tucked and hidden in the shadows of day, but I hold little more power than that cool, restful darkness, unless..." Mab let the sentence trail off, not wanting to let him know the price she would have to pay, the cruelty she must rain down upon the House of his friend, to walk in the sun.

"Unless?"

"Perhaps someday, if I have the strength,

this shall not always be. But for now, our time grows short and these precious moments should not be squandered with hopeless musings. Let us savor, instead, the time we have, even if it melts as a sugar violet in the mouth."

"The thought of parting tears at my soul as if ravens opened my chest and were feasting upon my heart," he said.

"Nay, gentle Meructio. Be not saddened that we must part, for parting only makes the reunion sweeter."

"A sweet reunion is nothing compared to the bliss of never parting."

She kissed him soundly, with the comfortable familiarity of a long kindred soul. "This I do swear to you that you and I shall never be parted during the night for as long as you walk this earth."

"I would gladly give up walking this earth if it meant that I could stay by your side without leaving."

"Do not wish such things that you do not know the price," she replied. The chill of her waking tomb called to her as false dawn began its rise. It told her to open her eyes from this dream and step back into the always waiting winter. She wept once more as she fought. Today she would stay on this earth invisible, today she would not leave Mercutio's side whether he could see her or could not. No matter what the cost to her strength, the passing years with him would be short, and she would not miss a breath.

"Why do you cry?" he asked.

"I must soon go. Please promise me that you will practice caution, that you will practice an even temper in the things that might cause your anger to rise."

"I shall," Mercutio smiled. "Who am I to vent my spleen when the humors of my blood runs so warm?"

She leaned over and kissed him. "Do not forget my love."

And as the first rays of the morning woke the day, she disappeared, her sparkling eyes and brilliant smile the last thing he saw before his eyes opened and found himself not Mab's palace, but his own room, and he was left to wonder if it was real or all just a dream.

Chapter Twenty-Seven

Tybalt sat at his desk, the wax seal pressed against the letter. He turned and handed it to the servant at his side.

"Deliver this to Romeo. Tarry not. Tell not a soul who it came from and to whom you deliver it to. Your life does depend upon it. Prince Escales has declared that any who is seen fighting in the street shall die, and I shall not be found a maker of distress to Prince Escales or Lord Capulet."

The servant bowed and left without a word.

Tybalt walked over to his window and stared down at the waking world. "But that which happens in the unseen streets shall trouble not the prince or my kinsman. If they only knew what danger lies in letting this insult pass without rebuke. One half of Faunus's prophecy has come to pass. A Montague welcomed into the House of Capulet. I have trained to become the greatest swordsman ever lived. As my patron Queen Mab advised, I shall rid this world of this boil before this boil festers and rids the world of me."

He stood from his desk and strapped his sword to his side, and prepared to walk out to greet either life or death as it might come.

Chapter Twenty-Eight

Mab watched Mercutio and Benvolio as they lounged in the town square. Though the sun was not high, the day was already warm, and threatened to be unbearable by the time it reached its height. She could not speak to Mercutio, she could not more than watch. She had found a shadow left from the night before and clung there like a shipwrecked sailor to a rock, all the while watching as the tide moved in.

"Where the devil should Romeo be?" asked Mercutio, looking about the streets. "Came he not home last night?"

"Not to his father's. I spoke with his man,"

replied Benvolio, holding his head steady so that the effects of the revelries might not cause him to be sick.

Mercutio smiled with rueful wisdom. "Ah, that Rosaline. She torments him so. He will surely go mad."

"Did you hear that Tybalt, one of Capulet's kinsman, sent a letter to Romeo's house?"

Mercutio sat up and looked at Benvolio, all artifice of ease gone. "A challenge, on my life," said Mercutio grimly.

"Romeo will answer it," replied Benvolio, his brutish ways seeing only one course.

"Any man that can write may answer a letter." He spat out a pomegranate seed. "The boy does not stand a chance against Tybalt's sword. I curse that I should have allowed you to accompany me to the masque. That I had kept my friendship with the Capulets confined to my own heart, Tybalt might not be hunting my friend in the streets."

"Nay, Romeo will give answer Tybalt. He will not back down."

"Alas poor Romeo! He is already dead," said Mercutio. "He is a mere boy destroyed by the foul looks of a woman. And you think he is a man to encounter Tybalt?"

"Why, what is Tybalt?" asked Benvolio dismissively.

Mercutio shook his head. "More than prince of cats, I can tell you. Oh, he seems a captain of compliments, but his sword picks up his cutting when his silver tongue is done. He plays the fop, but his limp wrist thrusts a rapier through the heart just as well as the steel-fisted hand of any bravado. Better, even. Why, he even introduced a new thrust, naming it the punto reverso, which is quite the rage at court."

"The what?"

"Punto reverso. Bah. A curse on him, to make killing the fashionable sport of those refined political dandies, men who will never swipe their blade outside a dueling field. They make mockery of the soldier as they prance and demand for blood, claiming honor and insult for matters that do not matter."

"You sound a bitter man. Did any at court ever call upon you demanding satisfaction?"

"The only courtly demands for satisfaction

that ever caused my sword to rise came from the fairer sex. While I might raise a legion to bear witness to the skill of my thrust and the punto reverso put to better use, there is some honor I will protect."

Benvolio grabbed his friend's arm. "Here comes Romeo."

"Oh, look upon his face," groaned Mercutio. "We shall have to put up with him extolling the virtues of whatever maid he landed. Be she a troll or a hag, she will seem to him Venus and us reluctant disciples for not making offerings at the foot of this new altar. How now, Romeo?"

Romeo gave a bow and threw himself upon the steps beside them. "Good morrow to you both."

"You disappeared last evening. Glad to see you well," answered Mercutio.

"Ah, if you only knew the depths of my wellness..."

"Speak no more!" said Mercutio, stopping his words before they came. "I am sure you have dug it deep enough to tap into the spring of love with a raging flow to quench the thirst of all Verona. Forgive me, I shall drink my wine."

"Chide me not, Mercutio. This fair lady is different! Oh, that you could see her!"

"Nay, a friend's eyes are best kept away from such temptations, for what if, upon looking, I see the virtues you extol and make a play to make her mine? No, no, Romeo. Keep your council to yourself and both you and I shall be the happier for it."

A rotund woman with chins aplenty waddled into the market square. She called out loudly in a voice like glass upon a slate, "Romeo? Is one of you Romeo?"

Mercutio grabbed Romeo by the shoulders. "Romeo! Why did you not say? So lovely! So fair! And you sought to keep her from me? For shame. For shame! My mistake, indeed. Dear Romeo, do tell me of the evening you spent together, locked in love's embrace. Tell me of your passion and how even dying shall not part thee."

"Romeo!" the nurse cried.

"It is not she. She is the nurse of my love," explained Romeo.

"She nurses your love? Well, good wishes to you, my friend. May your love suckle on the teat of her largess and grow stronger day by day."

"Gentlemen, can any of you tell me where I may find the young Romeo?" asked the Nurse coming to pause beside them.

"I am he," spoke Romeo.

Mercutio drew Romeo and the nurse close together. "I shall leave you to your discourse. Who am I to inhibit the unfolding of affection which burns so bright between you? Romeo, shall I see you at your father's home for dinner?"

Romeo practically pushed him on his way. "I shall see you later, my friend."

As Mercutio and Benvolio left the square, the nurse asked, "Who was that man?"

"A gentleman that loves to hear himself talk, and will speak more in a minute than he will stand to in a month," replied Romeo.

Mab followed Mercutio and Benvolio and the nurse's prattle faded into the gentle hum of the city. As they strolled, Mercutio yawned.

Benvolio asked, "Tired yet, in the middle of the morning? Did you not come home apace? Or did you find some other cunning distraction which kept you out of bed?"

"Aye," said Mercutio. "The sweetest distraction that a man can have, but I'm afraid it was all a dream."

"No lady fair scooped you up and asked you to make the dance?"

"When I left thee... it is strange that I cannot remember traveling home. It was as if I found the doorway to another world..."

"The drink did play tricks with your mind."

"Indeed, indeed, there is no other reason or rhyme." He smile. "Yet, if such dreams were true, I would ask never to wake, and would enjoy swimming in the sweetness of their taste."

"And what did you dream upon?"

"A woman. Who else? But an otherworldly beauty, either an angel without wings or a devil sent to ensnare me. Either case, she trapped me true."

"Ah, but to have such dreams."

"Indeed, especially when the waking brings

no peace."

"No peace? And here I brought such pleasant company."

"Benvolio, the clanging in your ears and turning of your stomach has turned your face green and not with envy for last night's sport. Still," said Mercutio, gripping his friend's arm, "it is good to have company. I have a strange foreboding about this day, an unnatural disquiet, and I am glad of your friendship."

"Do you still fret over the letter from Tybalt? Do you yearn for a love note from his courtly hand?"

"You have found me out, good Benvolio! Too long has he looked longingly upon my friends with never a glance towards me. I am jealous of his roving eye. The depths of your perception do you justice, my man. When you tire of the courts of Verona, we should set you up telling fortunes in a gypsy camp to blushing maids who know not their hearts. Or perhaps as Ambassador to France!"

"Here, let me buy you a drink and toast to your broken heart."

"Much more like to your broken head."

"Head or heart, no matter, the drink will cure them both."

Benvolio motioned to a seller, but Mercutio stopped as if torn. "We should go to my kinsman, Prince Escales, to make a report of Tybalt's threat. If only we had knowledge, not conjecture, of the contents inside. Such strangeness to this day! You would not solicit more than an understanding 'Indeed' if you were to tell me the heavens had switched the hours and ghosts walked at noon and midnight was the most mundane portion of the day."

"Fie! It is but the strangeness of some lingering dream, seeing enemies in the shadows when there are none. Let me buy you that drink and see if your disquietude stays."

Mercutio stood, torn between actions and then smiled. "I am a man of science, and if spirits may dispel this spirit, I am willing to put the hypothesis to the test."

"Come, my friend! Let us go inside and see what bottled joys give us knowledge and insight to our days."

Chapter Twenty-Nine

The afternoon heat had settled thickly, chasing away any cool happiness from the passing hours. All that was left was to endure until the sun fell once more upon the west horizon and the air could move again.

Mab sat as silent sentry as time slipped by both Benvolio and Mercutio, now resting from their tavern trip and dipping their hands in the bubbling fountain in the center of the square. She watched as observant as an artist who would later paint the scene from memory, capturing every movement with loving attention, the tilt of Mercutio's head, the turn of his cheek, etched as if an engraving in her mind.

So fixed was she, so enraptured with the life of her lover, that she did not see or hear the approach of cloven hooves.

"Why do you walk the day, you shade of evening's pleasure?" asked Faunus, looking at Mab as she clung to the shadows.

"I prithy, leave me be," she murmured. "My business is none of yours."

"That is so strange," replied Faunus. "For by the sun, I do believe that it is."

"I do not reflect your light today, Faunus. I come not for politics or pandering. Let me alone. I have no power. None can see me save you. I kindly ask that you let me remain here, invisible, to rest in these visions of day."

"Kindly ask? When have you not demanded and railed? It is as if the world has stopped spinning upon its axis. Tell me true and I shall consider your request — what inspired this change?"

She held no power here. Faunus need only grab her arm and yank her into the sun to banish her away. And so she confessed, "I orbit another star in the heavens."

"It is written in the sky that you and I shall spin around each other until time itself falls from exhaustion."

"No more," Mab replied, staring at the man whose gravitational pull had lifted her to another sun. "No more shall I play the part of moon to your heavenly body. I shall not be your balance of dark to light."

"This is quite a different tune to come from the throat of such a familiar nightingale."

"I have learned a new song from a morning lark who chose to sing to me."

"I should like to meet this bird and see if we are of the same feather."

"I do swear his plumage is quite different from your own."

"Think he more handsome than I?"

"Indeed, without compare."

"Think he more witty than I?"

"His tongue has no match."

"Think he more clever than I?"

"His mind knows no equal."

"Unfortunately, yours is not on par," said Faunus. "If so, you would know to hold your tongue, to whisper sweet flatteries to soothe my ego, bruised and injured. Instead, you hurl stones to make the wounds deeper, and deeply wounded, I must return them to you in kind."

"There is no insult you can hurl at me, no crime you might commit against my person that would cause me harm," she said dismissively. "You do not frighten me, old friend."

Faunus looked at the men now resting upon the steps. "But I know what you want. I know what you desire. And I know that there is something afoot. Whatever it is that you seek to create and defend, I shall dismantle piece by piece until nothing but rubble remains."

Mab stilled as he spoke, his words bringing back the chill to her heart which was once so warm. "This does not concern you, Faunus."

"I am afraid if some creature is causing your eye to seek the politics of day, to roam the streets, lurking in the shadows where the sun cannot touch, it is indeed my duty to thwart your efforts. You would return the kindness, I am sure, if I were to visit you at midnight and take a hand in the dreams you have spun."

"There are no dreams here, Faunus. Only lives that must be lived."

"Life itself is but a dream."

"Dreams can sometimes seem more real than this existence of flesh and blood, but these in this square seek out the night for their dreams and spend their days in human toil. None of which you see bears my touch. I stand only as silent witness and am no more threat to your domain than the passing breeze."

"But the breeze may become a wind and tear up an orchard before the harvest fruit brought in. The dreams that I create when their eyes are open, when they ruminate and spin on wealth and love are stronger than those images you lovingly plant when their eyes are closed and promise them the same gift," Faunus needled. "Do you long for this power to rule in the day?"

"Nay, Faunus, for how often do those same people tire of the world you give them and yearn for the gentleness of my embrace, turning to me to heal their wounds and soothe away their worries so that each morning they awake feeling lighter and without care?" asked Mab. "What more could I desire? I come not today to challenge thee."

"Since when have you been interested in the effects your night visitations have on these mortals? You and I both know you only draw them dreams to give your existence purpose."

"No, Faunus," she said, shaking her head, "that is no longer true. It might have been when I was a young thing in the world, but no more. My eyes have aged, I have aged, and no longer do I serve the master of self. I see that love is a force and from the lowest child to the highest lady, they both cry themselves to sleep at its breaking until my darkness overcomes them. It is only I who can heal their heart. I have seen this now, and I shall do my duty to see it through to the end. No more."

"You speak too much, again, Queen Mab," spoke Faunus. "You may believe your actions are nothing but duty, nothing but tidying up the unpleasant day. What I am afraid you do deny is that this is the beginning and only the fall will bring the end. Even if you do not wish to see the events that shall soon unfold, it does not matter, for I shall hold your face and pry your eyes so that you may not look away. You have shown me that you do not have the feet to march in this battle, so I shall out step you and see this tragedy to its end. Whether 'tis the House of Montague or Capulet that shall emerge the victor matters not. It is the game that keeps the days from growing too long. It is the change of mortal players that gives flavor to our feast. If you have lost the taste... why, it matters not to me, for I shall eat your helping in addition to my fill. I shall sup upon the delicacies of passion and bloodshed. I shall not rest until I have cracked the bones and sucked the marrow of their life."

Mab became very still as Faunus's words landed, the madness in his eyes filling her with dread. "This does not have to be."

Faunus reached down and poured his energy into the square until the air around Mercutio shimmered hot and unbearable.

"We made a wager. Two champions fueled with kindness to lead to the end of our bitter feud. House-to-House and hand-to-hand, they shall. And from this, you may rest happy in your victory, for I believe I shall let the House of Montague fall. Losing this game to you, Mab, already tastes sweeter than even the dreams you plant."

"Willingly lose to me? What sort of trick is this?" asked Mab in desperation. "It is no longer a wager when one decides not to play, for upon its breaking such promises become the wind and nothing more than words scattered into the silence."

"Nay, you are mistaken, Mab. A wager is a contract, and no amount of protest may break its binding. The House of Montague will fall just as you have always wanted, and the devastation of victory shall show you the error of your ways."

"I shall not play, Faunus!"

"A simple death, a brawl in the streets, that is how it all begins," said Faunus smiling and looking towards her love. "Did you not see this in your basin? I warned you to stay away.

By your very involvement, a careless word or two, you have played your part well, becoming the catalyst which shall cause all the death that you have just now grown to abhor."

"Forget the binding, Faunus. Let them live."

"And why should I do that?" he asked.

"Because I am commanding you."

"That is not reason enough not to start."

"Because I am asking you."

"We are far beyond asking, my queen."

"Because I am begging," she whispered.

"Nay, queen, it is quite too late for that, too."

"Why are you doing this?"

"For sport," Faunus replied without a trace of a smile upon his face.

Oh, that her heart would harden into ice once more, she thought. Oh, that she could forget the warmth that she had felt, that she could close her eyes to the light and love which she found upon the face of a simple human. But there sat Mercutio beside his friend, relaxed in blissful ignorance. The nearness of him was now was a chasm of a thousand leagues and he was so far beyond her warning touch.

"The summer sun is warm, enough to make the tempers of young men rise," said Faunus. "So it begins."

Benvolio leaned over the fountain and dipped his kerchief in the water, dabbing it on the back of his neck. "Good Mercutio, let us retire. The day is hot, the Capulets are in the streets and if we meet, we shall not escape a brawl; for now, these hot days, is the mad blood stirring."

Mab willed that good Mercutio might hear and heed Benvolio's words, that they might remind him of a promise made in her bed. This tragedy might be sidestepped. But Faunus smiled and with a wave of his hand, the heat of the day became even more oppressive.

Mercutio shook his head at Benvolio. "You are like one of those fellows who enters a tavern and throws down his sword, swearing, 'I have no need of this!' and by the time he drinks his second cup, pulls his sword on the barkeeper for no reason at all."

"Am I like such a fellow?"

"Come, come, you are as hot a fellow in your moods as any in Italy, and as soon moved to be moody, and as soon moody to be moved."

"And what to?"

"You will quarrel with a man who has a hair more, or a hair less, in his beard than you have. You will quarrel with a man for cracking nuts for no other reason than because he has hazel eyes. You have quarreled with a man for coughing in the street because he has awoken a dog who slept in the sun. Did you not have a falling out with a tailor for wearing his new doublet before Easter? With another for tying his new shoes with old ribbon? And yet you will tutor me to keep from quarrelling? Ha!"

But their toothless spat was interrupted as the Capulet kinsman, Tybalt, came into the square. His singular purpose made clear with his hand upon the hilt of his sword and the armed friends at his side.

"By my head, here come the Capulets," said Benvolio.

Mercutio leaned back and closed his eyes to the sun. "By my heel, I care not."

Time seemed to slow its course as Mab remembered her words to Tybalt - to strike down a Montague before he had the chance to strike first. She hoped he had taken her advice not to heart. Oh, if she could but withdraw those words. She looked at Benvolio and wondered how such a clumsy lad could bring about the fall of such a man as Tybalt. Or would Tybalt make the first blow and trick the fates to let him live?

"What trouble does this Tybalt mean?" Mab begged to Faunus. "You must turn aside this fate. These are not games. These are not the ways to pass the days."

"Why do you fret? Tybalt is a champion of your House! Quite the fetching savior of the Capulets and a more handsome protector of her honor Verona could not dream to want. What worries you? He, this creature who falls beneath your protection from a promise made long ago, needs only to be slayed, and the House of Montague will no longer be."

"Let Tybalt be slayed, then," she whispered

looking at her Mercutio. "Let him fall without fight. Only let this cup pass and this game be done."

"Nay, Mab," whispered Faunus. "For you see, I have my own champion, whom just the taste of kindness will cast aside his peaceable ways and cause him to fight to the death to defeat this man."

"Tybalt needs not defeat. He needs only to walk away."

Tybalt looked into the courtyard, scanning the crowd for the Montague colors. His eyes fell upon Benvolio seated by the fountain with Mercutio, and waved his friends to fall in behind. "Follow me close, for I will speak to them." Stepping boldly across the courtyard, he bowed, but never let his eyes leave their face. "Gentlemen, a word with one of you."

Mercutio looked upon him and Mab knew the thoughts that flitted across the face of this lighthearted soul, whose courage was forged on the fields of battle. She saw that he knew Tybalt sought out his friend. She saw that he knew if the two were joined, Tybalt's sword would end Romeo, for this lover was no soldier and knew not how to fight for his life.

Mab willed Mercutio to go to the prince, to let this meaningless moment of great matter pass, but the wine and the heat had gone to his head, the seriousness of the threat gave him courage. Tybalt wanted a fight, and if it be Romeo or the clumsy brute Benvolio, neither would escape, and Mercutio understood this truth. So instead, he rose, ready to take the brunt of Tybalt's ire in the hope that both might live to see another day.

"And but one word with one of us?" said Mercutio, shielding Benvolio from sight. "Couple it with something. Make it a word and a blow."

"You shall find me apt enough to that, sir, and you will give me occasion," replied Tybalt, not backing down from the threat. "Mercutio, you consort with Romeo—"

"Consort!" Mercutio laughed. "You make us sound like minstrels, ready to play for the pleasure for whatever foolish lord taps his feet. Well, if I am a minstrel, my song is filled with discordant chords, and if you wish to change the tune, come and take my fiddlestick." He placed his hand upon the hilt of his rapier. "Here is that which shall make you dance."

Benvolio came between them holding out his hands. "You talk here in public on the crowded street. Either withdraw to some private place to reason out your grievances or else depart. Here all eyes gaze on us."

"Men's eyes were made to look, and let them gaze," said Mercutio in warning, protecting his friend and daring Tybalt to strike a kinsman of Verona's prince. "I will not budge."

At that moment, the fair-haired Romeo entered into the square, blissfully unaware of the tragedy that was about to befall. He seemed to float rather than walk and bore the markings of love's blinders which kept a man's eyes upon his lady and from seeing any of the world beyond. A smile was on his face as if no woe could touch his gladness and he seemed anxious to get to his friends to tell them of fortune's touch.

Faunus looked at Mab. "My champion has arrived. And so the world ends."

Faunus removed the vial and uncorked the stopper. He threw it in the air blowing it towards Romeo. As it struck, Romeo inhaled the happiness and wellbeing which seemed to mirror the feelings found already in his heart.

Mab wished she could reach out and, pressing her hands upon Romeo's shoulders, move him back to where he came from, but his feet continued steadily on, finding joy in the sunlight and seeking not the shadows of her intervention.

Tybalt looked over. Smiling, he turned from Mercutio to this boy. "Well, peace be with you, sir. Here comes my man."

"Your man? He does not wear your livery," said Mercutio, trying to keep Tybalt's attention. "But lead the way to the dueling ground instead this ambush in the street and indeed he will face you there, for he is such a man."

Tybalt would not be distracted by Mercutio's words and called, "Romeo, the hate I bear towards you can afford no better term than this—thou art a villain!"

Romeo stopped, suddenly aware of the

faces and tempers he had stumbled into. He placed his hands up in peace and spoke out in soothing tones, "Tybalt, there are ties which bind us that cause me not to answer the insult you give. Villain am I none. Therefore, farewell. You know me not."

Tybalt, thinking back to the prophecy of ages ago called out, "Boy, this shall not excuse the injuries that thou hast done me; therefore turn and draw."

He ran at Romeo, sword in hand, and Romeo sped to get away. Unarmed, he used his tongue to fight the madness which had seized Juliet's cousin. "I do protest, I never injured you! And so, good Capulet, which name I tender as dearly as my own, be satisfied!"

But Tybalt would not and he advanced upon Romeo as if to force him to find a sword to draw or die a coward in the street. He pointed his bare blade upon Romeo as if to run him through. Romeo stood with his hands held up in peaceful surrender as Tybalt's anger grew.

Mab watched in horror as Mercutio

unsheathed his own rapier to protect his weaker friend. He stepped between Tybalt and Romeo and challenged, "Tybalt, you rat-catcher, will you walk?"

Tybalt looked upon Mercutio, gentle Mercutio, friend of both Houses, in confusion. "What wouldst thou have with me?"

"Good king of cats, I want nothing but the first of your nine lives. You may then have your other eight to do with as you will. Move your sword away from this foolhardy boy and face the man before you before I give you not a choice."

Tybalt turned his blade upon his new target, knowing that Mercutio posed no danger. The old god had warned him of a Montague, and Mercutio was not one. Tybalt knew this was not the day that he had been preparing for his entire life. "I am for you."

"We shall kill them with kindness, shall we Mab?" whispered Faunus. "Present thy champion, for the match point is upon us. Choose who shall protect the House of Capulet."

But Mab had drunk the kindness and there was no champion to be had.

Faunus leaned once more towards Romeo, causing him to leap into the fray, pleading with honesty and goodwill, the taste of Capulet's goodness still upon his lips. "Gentle Mercutio, put thy rapier up!"

But Mercutio would not be swayed.

"Come, sir, give me that thrust that I have heard so much about in court," Mercutio taunted at Tybalt before giving in to the attack.

Mab could feel Faunus's heat in every word as his fiery influence sped their blades and gave strength to each blow. In horror, she watched, impotent and unable to provide protection, only witness. Capulet's kindness was within her and it burned bitterly to know that even when she thought she was out-foxing Faunus, she was two steps behind his plans. She could not pass the kindness to Tybalt now to stay his hand. Instead, she saw her love, Mercutio, defend himself. He seemed fixed on disarming Tybalt, to answer Tybalt's insults with a lesson in respect, but

Tybalt was not a man to let his ego be bruised. No, indeed, correction was a crime worth retaliating in his book.

If only she had some cruelty to give to Mercutio, wept Mab, to match the bloodlust that pounded in the veins of his foe.

"Draw, Benvolio," Romeo begged his lumbering friend, "beat down their weapons."

But Benvolio hung back, unwilling to break the prince's decree, even if it meant the life of his most worthy friend.

Romeo ran between Tybalt and Mercutio, trying to stay their bare blades with his bare body. "Gentlemen, for shame, forbear this outrage! Tybalt, Mercutio, the prince expressly hath forbidden bandying in Verona streets. Hold, Tybalt! Good Mercutio!"

Mercutio pushed Romeo aside to get the boy out of harm's way. Instead of gratitude, Romeo ran forward, hugging Mercutio's arms to his side in order to pull him from the fight. In that moment of horrible distraction, neither saw Tybalt's thrust. From beneath Romeo's arm, Tybalt's blade found its mark in Mercutio's side.

"I am hurt," said Mercutio. Blood spread across his doublet as if red ink spilled across a virgin page.

Mab felt her lover's pain as if it was her own heart that had been run through, but her cries of horror carried no more weight than the wind. She braced herself, the sight of Mercutio's crimson life calling like a siren's invitation to dash herself upon the rocks. She willed herself not to rush to his side. She was trapped in the prison of shadows with the sun as her jailor. One step into the unshaded square and she would wake in the icy prison of her reality, never again to see her love.

Tybalt stiffened, the madness of Faunus finally lifted, to see what he had done. In horror, his eyes grew wide, knowing that this, slaying the Prince's kinsman, meant his own death. He motioned to his friends and they fled.

Mercutio's hands touched his wound and he gasped in anger and in sadness. "A plague on both your houses! I am sped. Is he gone and hath nothing?"

"What, art thou hurt?" asked Benvolio,

helping Mercutio as he slid to the ground.

Mercutio lifted his hand and showed him the blood. "Ay, ay, a scratch, a scratch; marry, 'tis enough."

"Courage, man," said Romeo, trying to will the wound to be much smaller than it was, "the hurt cannot be much."

"No, it is not so deep as a well, nor so wide as a church door; but it is enough, it will serve." He began laughing, though his face twisted in agony. "Ask for me tomorrow and you shall find me a grave man. I am peppered, I warrant, for this world."

A spasm shook his body and he gasped. He shouted in his pain the words that Mab screamed from the shadows. "A plague on both your houses! Zounds, a dog, a rat, a mouse, a cat, to scratch a man to death! A braggart, a rogue, a villain, that fights by the book of arithmetic!" Mercutio looked up at Romeo and, begging, looked into his eyes for answers. "Why the devil came you between us? I was hurt under your arm."

Romeo, his mouth filled with secrets he could not reveal, with a heart destroyed by the moment of peace it was trying to give, could only answer back, "I thought it all for the best."

Another wave caused poor Mercutio's body to clench and convulse. Laughing once again as his face became ashen grey, he held his arms to his other friend. "Help me into some house, Benvolio, or I shall faint."

Benvolio gently placed his friend's arm around his own neck and lifted him. Mercutio cried out and paled, his knees buckled unable to bear his weight. He shouted, "A plague on both your houses! They have made worms meat of me. I have it, and soundly too! Your houses!"

Faunus's laughter echoed through the square, delighting in his victory. Mab fell to the ground, wracking sobs heaving in her chest.

"Why mourn you so, Queen Mab? This tragedy is your own, every event a direct result of your meddling and schemes," Faunus said. He gave her a wink. "What sport. We should play again."

And then he disappeared.

Chapter Thirty

Mab stood in the doorway as they took her love to couch, resting him gently upon the cushions as he bled.

She knew he could not see her. The daylight made it so, fading her corporal appearance to nothing but motes within a sunbeam. But she would stay until the end. She would not let one breath of his slip away without bearing witness. She would remember, even though she felt her heart might break with each gasp. Indeed, it did break. She wanted to curse Romeo and Tybalt and all the foolish humans who had looked on at the violence in the street. But she could not. For she knew that it was her fault. It was the steady march of one hundred years of unkindness which now took her love forever from the earth, his smile never to grace the sunrise, his laugh never to fill the air. She had learned to love too late, and the mistakes were all her own.

And yet, when his eyes opened he seemed to see her, for they softened and for a moment appeared almost glad. She stepped forward into the darkened room, unable to keep away. He whispered, "Queen Mab... have you a hazelnut shell to come and bear me away?"

"Do not leave us, good Mercutio!" urged Benvolio.

But Mercutio had eyes for none other than his queen.

"How you seems to shine in the sunlight," he smiled. "How your darkness seems to almost glow."

"Forgive me, my love! Forgive me!" she whispered. "I would risk all to save you. I should destroy my very world if I could lift so much as a finger to come to your aid. And yet, I cannot. Forgive me for being powerless and for leaving you alone to face your death!"

The tears streamed down her face, tears from one whose heart had once hardened to ice, but now melted for one human.

He reached out his hands, as if to wipe those tears away. His friend, Benvolio, reached out to grasp it, thinking he was reaching for someone else.

But Mab knew who he yearned for, whose perfect soul had finally matched his.

"What dreams we could have had," he whispered to her.

And she knew an immortal existence was not worth a moment without him there at her side.

"Tell him to - shutter the windows," she spoke.

Mercutio turned to Benvolio. "Draw the curtains my friend, for indeed the curtains are being drawn upon me."

"You shall not die..."

"Please, as my one request. Into darkness I entered this world, crying a newborn's mewling cries as the midwife guided me from the dark safety of my mother's womb into a room warm and shuttered. And now I return to the quiet darkness. And it is within this warm and shuttered room that I wish to rest this final rest, guarded from the world lest I make a mewling cry once more for my mother."

Benvolio stood and walked to the window.

Mab stepped closer, the shadows adding such a little strength to her footsteps, but every ounce of power she gobbled up as a prisoner with stolen rations.

"I see you much clearer, Mab," he smiled.

"Do not speak this way!" said Benvolio with wetness upon his cheeks.

Mab knelt beside Mercutio and stroked his face, her fingers hungry for the warmth of his skin, of his human imperfections. Of the hair that grew upon his face each day. The scars and bumps and lines, whose marrings made him extraordinary and more exquisitely beautiful than all the perfection of the faerie.

"How cold I grow," Mercutio spoke.

"Do not leave!" said Benvolio, kneeling at Mercutio's other side. But Mercutio did not turn his head.

"You shall grow colder still, my love," she said.

Mercutio smiled. "I shall welcome the darkness's embrace like your arms, greet the black as much as the night when lovers might murmur secrets that cannot bear the light."

"You may come with me," Queen Mab whispered. "You may come, but it shall cost you a terrible price."

His eyes became clear for just a moment as he looked at her, listening to the words she had to say.

"But if you come, never shall you rest in the fields of heaven. Indeed," she confessed, "if I had to choose again, I would allow myself to slip quietly into the netherworld and leave this Earth far behind. But my heart makes me selfish. My heart betrays both you and I and urges me to speak and convince you to choose this unwise path. I cannot stop my heart! If you wish to stay, you may come with me, and together, we shall watch o'er the dreamworld, guiding those who slumber to the morning light. You may choose. But know that whatever you choose, my love, for you is forever," she wept.

Mercutio reached up and touched her cheek. "Of course I will stay with you, my love."

And then he breathed his last.

"He is dead!" cried Benvolio.

Queen Mab watched as Benvolio raced out of doors and heard him cry, "Romeo, Romeo, brave Mercutio's dead!"

She buried her face against Mercutio's chest.

"Here comes the furious Tybalt back again," Benvolio continued.

"Come, my love," she whispered to Mercutio. "We cannot dally here with the blood lust of these foolish young men about."

The sound of swords crashed withal, the grunts and thrashing of a man whose heart had been destroyed by the fall of his friend. She felt Romeo's blade plunge into the heart of Tybalt, for as it struck true, so it struck the keystone that kept the House of Montague together.

As Tybalt gasped, each breath becoming

weaker, the House of Montague fell. Romeo's murderous shame dashed its glory upon the flagstones in crimson red. And with each crumbling stone, the strength of Mab returned. Though Tybalt died, the House of Capulet rose, and contract between she and Tybalt held, banishing the curse which barred Mab from the day. No longer bound, she stood whole and healthy though the sun was in the sky, and laid claim to the power which had been stolen from her.

Chapter Thirty-One

The room was dark and cold. She wished it could be as warm as the summer sun, but alas. Mercutio lay in her bed, the bearskin rug he might once have needed to stay warm draped across his body. He would never again feel the need for wraps or coats. Indeed, he would never have need for warmth inside a lover's arms. Cold would be his eternal tomb, just as it was for her.

His eyes fluttered, his dark pupils wide as they adjusted to the light in her snowy chamber. She knelt beside him and clasped his hand to her heart.

"You are awake, my love."

He turned to her slowly, as if his body was not used to the sensation of movement. He blinked again and whet his lips, a strangely human movement for one who had left that world.

"What place am I?" he asked, his hand running over his side where the sword had pierced him, puncturing his mortality and allowing his life to flood away. The skin was smooth as a newborn, no scar or wound to mar his perfect skin.

Queen Mab smoothed back his hair, her pale hand so white against his black curls. "Such dreams we shall have... did you not say that my love?"

Mercutio nodded slowly, as if thought was being filtered through a veil of remembrance.

"It was your choice, not mine," the Queen whispered. "I despise myself for taking you, knowing what life I offer. You are in my winter, in my waking days. There is no more life than here, but hopefully it will be life enough for you."

Mercutio reached up and stroked her cheek. "I would rather be here with you than in any fields of heaven. Such a heaven would seem a hell without you. Do not look at me with such sadness, for I live thanks to your touch. Indeed, I believe I never truly lived before. This strangeness will fade, for you and I are together. Do not weep, my Queen."

He wiped away her tears.

She stared at the wetness as it sat upon his finger. "It shall freeze, as it always does, so cold within this chamber."

"But look," he smiled, showing her his hand, "it stays warm."

She gripped his hand. "It shall freeze."

Mercutio sat up. "You may have existed for a thousand years, my Queen, but I say you, too, have not lived until this moment. I say that you, too, shall discover an adventure that is far beyond your understanding, all based upon the touch of a forgotten drop of sadness." He kissed her palm and gripped it tight. "Now, my queen, you must tell me what happened after I remember no more."

"I brought you here."

"Yes, but what of my kinsmen? Of Romeo and Benvolio?"

She shook her head. "I am afraid that in his anger, Romeo sought revenge. His heart was cleft in twain, grieving for your loss."

Mercutio struggled to rise. "Then we must tell him that I live!"

"No," she said, placing her hand upon his chest and gently lowering him back to his pillow. She missed the way his heart used to beat. "No, my love."

"But why not? Bloodshed for blood shed makes mourners of us all. There is no joy in revenge, no taste of honeyed happiness found in the goblet of rogue justice served."

"These are mysteries the world still struggles with. These are lessons that they have been taught since the dawn of time and, yet, they still fight and die, as if without care, as if relishing the release from their mortal coil."

"I am coiled to spring, to save those I love. They should not die for me."

"Do you not understand the choice that you have made?" Queen Mab asked, the pain unable to stay behind its quiet mask of ice. "Do you not understand that when you chose to live by my side, you left behind the cares and worries of that world? We cannot become involved in the politics of man, for they are now nothing more than a dream."

"There will be a way," he continued. He placed a finger to her lips and silenced her with his touch. It seemed to still hold the final drops of warm mortal life, and she would not let her words chase such warmth away. Mercutio pulled her down and placed a kiss upon her forehead. "Worry that heavy brow of yours no more. If this is reality and the other a dream, I am content to never close my eyes again. Indeed, with you in my arms, everything beyond this bed could fall and fade and I would not know the difference. We shall sort the dealings of the weary world when you and I have wearied ourselves of one another and not a moment before. This I promise, my Mab."

He sealed his words with a comforting kiss, which deepened and lengthened as the promises gave way to the actions of truth.

But a sound rumbled outside as if coming thunder, though the sky was clear. Mab rose from Mercutio, not remembering the sound of a storm in all her years in this prison. She stepped out onto her balcony and the coldness descended as an ice storm. It bit at her skin, reminding her of who she was and what she stood for.

Though the unending night still surrounded her palace, standing in a beam of sun, sweating and panting stood her rival, Faunus. The look upon his eyes was one of bitter hatred, as if he might be able to burn her to ashes with his ire.

Queen Mab wrapped her arms around herself, shivering, and stared up at the sky.

"This is my realm!" she shouted. "Who dares disturb my borders?"

A sparkling beam of sunlight fell between the two demigods. And when the sun stuck, they found themselves in the presence of a real god.

"Juno," whispered Queen Mab.

"Juno," wheezed Faunus, scraping a bow upon the ground.

"SILENCE!" the goddess boomed.

Both Mab and Faunus held their tongues.

Juno stepped forward, her peacock trailing at her side. "Did you say that these were your borders, Mab?" she asked. "Did you pretend that in a place in which your eyes were open fell under your control?"

Her peacock let out a loud cry and flung his tail open to display his feathers.

Queen Mab bowed her head, her heart pounding. "It was my mistake, goddess."

"Indeed, a grave mistake," Juno said, regarding her with disdain. "I have word from Faunus that this is a repeat offense. He tells me you dabble in realms that are quite outside your borders, faerie."

Mab protested, "I abide by my duties to the humans I protect."

With a flick of her wrist, Juno opened a fan made by the cast off feathers of her bird. She glanced back knowingly at Faunus. "This duty includes destroying the House of Montague?"

"Nay," said Queen Mab, who did not raise her eyes from their fixed point on the ground. "That was a challenge posed by Faunus. He proposed a settlement to our feud. Any harm I gave to Montague was a mirror to the danger he posed to the House of Capulet, to those who come to me demanding my protection and care."

"She lies! Look at events! See how selflessness has guided my actions, placing the House of Montague at risk to try and preserve the peace! Her man slew the prince's kinsman, making Romeo hunger for revenge. And now the House of Montague falls, just as she always planned."

Mab's heart caught in her throat, thinking of Mercutio who lay within, seeing Faunus as if for the very first time. She shook her head slowly. "No. Faunus caused the death of those I had sworn to protect."

"Lies!" cried Faunus. "Lies she speaks! Though always the Montagues' keeper, I also took upon a boy from the House of Capulet when Mab's jealousies and rages placed him without a protector. Young Tybalt came to me when he was just a boy, remembering the old ways and bringing sacrifices to us gods. He prayed for long life and power. Alas, this man, this Mercutio that Mab has adopted for a pet, caused his death and downfall. She protects not the House of Capulet. She protects not the House of Montague. If not for Mab's interference, all would be alive today."

Juno looked at her two quarreling underlings, weighing out their truth and their life in measure against a feather weight scale.

"Look at how she flaunts the laws of mortals! Look within her bedchamber. You will find that she has even snatched this Mercutio from his natural end. And for what end? To be her immortal plaything? To bestow upon him the rights and privileges which are reserved for the gods?"

Juno looked upon Mab. "Is this true?"

"My heart could not let him die."

Juno paused, as if surprised by some strangeness in Mab's words. "Your heart?"

"Aye," replied Mab, the sigh of this simple word carrying the weight of a thousand speeches. "Please give me a chance to right these wrongs."

Juno looked at her closer. "Your face has changed, Queen Mab."

Mab had no idea why such a change would

cause such a goddess to change her mind. But it did.

Juno proclaimed, "I shall give you until the third day to return the House of Montague to glory. If the words you speak are true, not just your life, but the eternal life of this man you love, shall be forfeit."

"Thank you," Queen Mab whispered.

"Do not trouble me with your thanks!" Juno snapped back. "But as escrow to your goodwill, I take your love, Mercutio, and keep him for myself!"

"No!" Mab cried, even as Juno stretched out her arm and sent forth a calling into Mab's bedchambers. "No!" Mab cried once again, running in to where Mercutio lay and watching as he faded as sure as she herself faded whenever she walked in the sun.

"Set these things to right, Mab, or else never see his return," Juno spoke and with that, she stepped behind her peacock who fanned out his mighty tail. Like a trickster magician, Juno was gone.

Faunus's anguish disappeared and he fixed Mab with a knowing grin. He leered at her, rubbing his hands in delight. "Let the games begin again," said Faunus. "You played so well before."

Then he, too, disappeared.

Queen Mab sat down upon the cold bed, lost in the despair of her task. She stroked the pillow where the man she loved had just moments before softly laid his head. "I must cease the stones even as they tumble from the turrets. I must stop the foundations from their shaking though the earth beneath them trembles. I foolishly became my own champion, injured by kindness and weakened by these feelings of love." She looked into the mirror. "The House of Montague must not fall, else my Mercutio disappears forever. Such cruelty, such twists of fate which I could not see within my basin. My doom is of my own sentence. My heart breaking for the actions I must take, for I see clearly the path before me, the weight and terrible price of what I must engage in if he and I are to live. Oh, gentle Mercutio, the wounds I must bring to bear against thy friends and kinsmen hurt twice as much as the wounds I bring against

myself, but for you, I must bear them both."
She lay down upon the bedclothes which still
smelled of him, and clung to the knowledge
she would do anything for his return. She
closed her eyes in one world so that she might
wake in another.

Chapter Thirty-Two

Lord Capulet stood outside Prince Escales's palace and quietly hung his head so that, despite the day, none might see his sadness. The pain in his heart was for his nephew Tybalt, a hot-headed boy, but one who strived, one who would have indeed brought the House of Capulet to great heights and preserved the greatness of a long and powerful lineage.

But now? Now, he reflected, there was nothing, nothing but his daughter. He had no son to carry on his name, no male heir to protect the Capulet blood.

Oh, that he could kill Romeo with his own

two hands. Oh, if only Queen Mab had warned him of this. He had been so focused upon his daughter's inevitable betrayal, that he had not thought his nephew might be guilty of the greater sin—losing his life to a Montague.

"Already this and yet to know enough of the future that the cruelest blow, to be struck with a closed fist by my daughter, is still to come..."

"What is to come?" asked a cheerful voice.

Lord Capulet looked up, startled.

"You must forgive me," said Lord Capulet, clutching his heart, "You gave me a fright. I could have sworn that I was quite alone."

"My dear sir, I could not help but notice your distress," said the man. He walked out from behind a cart. He had brown curly hair and a brown beard. His chest was bare, but for a strap that cut across it, surely for holding a purse. Indeed, he pulled out some pipes and began to play. He must have been wearing hard shoes, Lord Capulet mused, because his feet made almost the sound of horses or goats stepping upon the cobblestones.

"Indeed, my grief is that which would level the heart of any man, and no man think him less than a man for grieving. My dear nephew has been slaughtered in the street."

The stranger gave a gasp in horror and motioned Lord Capulet to an overturned crate. "Sit, sir..."

"I am Lord Capulet."

The man bowed. "Even more so. Sit, my lord, and tell me of all your woes. You will not find a better ear in all of Verona. I shall get to the meat of it and perhaps see some solution to your pain."

"Nay, no one may ease this weight upon my heart. I wade not in the shallows. I am chest high in the depths of my anguish."

"Tut, tut. That is too much for one person to bear. And why did this happen, my lord?"

"I know not. I know not," he replied, waving his hand dismissively. "I only know that they did quarrel. But I was the one who put them in each other's path. I allowed the mongrel of a Montague into my home, why, just last night! I welcomed him as a guest! I shook his hand! And my nephew took it upon himself to dispense the rightful hospitality he felt was lacking in my home. Oh! If I had but listened... And now he is dead. I see the last of the Capulet male blood surrendered to the bloody altar of a centuries-old feud. I fear the cruelty to come and that which the Fates have in store."

"Nay, sir. The Fates are kind to those who love them. If you fear the weakening of your House you must strengthen it."

"I have only a daughter."

"Then marry her soon and marry her well. Let the shame of Tybalt's death hang on the House of Montague and use this moment to fill the emptiness they have left. Unite your child with one who will elevate your House to the glory that it once was and might have been. In a few years time, so many babies and grandchildren will bounce upon your knee, you'll scarce have leg for it. Trust me in this wisdom, for it was won over many a hard year."

"It is too soon for her to wed," he protested.

"Such decisions need not be made with haste. Merely think upon it. What suitor might wipe clean the sadness of the day and fill broken hearts with healing?"

"There was a cousin named Paris that Tybalt seemed to like..." Lord Capulet mused. The danger now passed, it seemed as if a natural solution to a problem that was plaguing him. "Paris came to visit me not yesterday. My, was it only yesterday? He made suit at our masque and my daughter Juliet was to receive him. After such terrible events and anguish, I did not even ask how she thought upon him."

"Seems as if a question a loving father might inquire," stated the strange man, picking his teeth with a pointed nail. "Go you to your daughter. Unite her with this Paris fellow, for I have heard of his exploits and wealth from low-and-far to high-and-low. See if her heart might be bent to his love. And if so, this daughter of your ruin shall become the angel of your salvation."

Lord Capulet nodded. "Your words are sound and fill this grieving man with hope.

Tonight is almost gone and her tears have not yet ceased. I cannot think of such a happy event on such a day of pain, but tomorrow I shall speak with her and let this moment fade from sorrow to joy."

Lord Capulet turned to thank the man, but when he looked, there was no one there. Lord Capulet rubbed his eyes. Though the sun still hung in the sky, he felt as if he had woken from a dream. His eyes were sandy and his heart strangely beat.

Slowly, he turned the way he came and began walking back towards his house.

Faunus watched as Lord Capulet went. Such a fascinating human, he thought, so willing to engage in whatever it took to secure what he felt he deserved. Faunus smiled. They seemed to be two of a kind and Faunus looked forward to being so much more than just an adviser.

No more would he be mere demigod, scraping at the feet of Jupiter and Juno. These humans with their power of adoration would crown him rightfully. They would bow down before him, and in doing so, turn him to a god. And why not? Such horrors they could avoid by worshipping him. Mab would no longer strangle their line, plaguing their dreams so that their days seemed full of woe.

Faunus thought of the marble statue they would carve of him, of the wreathes of flowers that they would lay at his feet. At the way the House of Capulet would teach their children and their children's children of his munificence and glory. They would be so grateful for his sound council. The plans he began a century ago by that theft of Mab's sacred bull were finally ripening and, at last, almost ready for the plucking.

But first, to County Paris. This Lord Capulet might still change his mind. Too easy tomorrows and tomorrows became the unfolding promises of days which never came. Faunus would send Paris to the Capulet house this very night and before the sun rose, a day would be set for a union so blessed, it would to make the gods smile.

Indeed, Faunus smiled.

Chapter Thirty-Three

Mab's eyes opened in her palace in Verona. The world was already deep into night and who knew what terrible events had come to pass since she walked this earth. She tried not to think of Mercutio and the last breaths he sighed so very close to this place. Mab let Juno's command temper her heart, allowed the fire of her words forge her resolve like a sword beneath the master's hammer, honing it for its singular purpose, knowing if she failed, she would never see her love again. It was not yet time for mourning.

In haste, she called for her chariot and made way to the Capulet house. The home was dark, almost all of it in slumber, except for a single light in a front receiving room. Mab flew to the open window to see what secrets were unfolding when the rest of the house was abed.

Inside, Lord and Lady Capulet were speaking to Paris.

"So yea or nay? Shall Juliet be my wife?" asked the young man sharply.

Mab's heart grew troubled, knowing this conversation was too soon, knowing that the good family Capulet would never have spoken of such things without unnatural influence, and yet, there they stood, unfolding.

Lord Capulet paced beside his window, staring at the sky as he spoke, "I have not had time to speak to my daughter. She is grieving even now for her kinsman Tybalt. The hour is late and the moon in the sky. If you had not come, I would be in bed myself. Let us speak another day."

Paris did not seem to understand the weariness in the man's voice. He did not seem to hear the pain and anguish wracking this man's soul. No, indeed, he seemed to be controlled by one whose influence was much greater than kindness and love. With a sharp edge, Paris did command, "Lady Capulet, please take me to your daughter. I will have her happy answer and her joyful hand and, in doing so, will aid her in casting aside this grief."

Mab recoiled, realizing it was the dream she had planted foolishly in Paris just days ago which still held its talons in his soul. It told him to speak and demand when the moment would be better served by temperance. Once more she felt the weight of her fault in this. It was hers and no one else's.

Lady Capulet tried to reason with him. "I will, and I will know her answer for you early tomorrow, but tonight she is filled with woe and tears."

Lord Capulet turned to Paris, exhausted and seeing that the night would not come to an end. "County Paris, I will speak with her. She will abide by my will, I do not doubt. She shall be yours. This I will command! Indeed, I shall set forth the wheels this very moment. Wife? Talk to her of Paris's love. Tell her the wedding shall be Wednesday next—But, soft! what day is this?"

"Monday, my lord," said Paris.

"Monday! Well, Wednesday is too soon. Thursday. Let it be on Thursday. Wife, tell her that on Thursday she shall be married to this noble earl." Lord Capulet turned to Paris and asked, "Will you be ready? Do you like this haste? We shall keep the celebration small. If we make too merry so soon after Tybalt slain, it might be seen that we cared not as deeply for him as we do. Therefore we'll have some half a dozen friends, no more. Perhaps a dozen. Or two. But that is a matter for later. What say you to Thursday?"

"My lord, my heart wishes that Thursday was tomorrow, but I wait knowing the day's arrival will be made that much sweeter for the longing of it," Paris smiled.

"Well get you gone. On Thursday be it, then," said Lord Capulet with a dismissive wave.

Paris nodded in acquiescence.

"Go you to Juliet in the morrow," commanded Lord Capulet to his lady.

"Prepare her, wife, against this wedding day." He turned back again to Paris. "Farewell, my lord." Then he called loudly to his servants, "Light to my chamber, ho! It is so very late that we may call the day early by and by. Good night."

Mab stood as the three exited the room until she was all alone. Her thoughts tumbled in her head. If Juliet married Paris, she would live. But what of the House of Montague? What of this boy, Romeo, who once had been her Mercutio's friend? The House had fallen from his shame and time would not restore them to glory. The last of the Montague line would die from despair, waiting in exile for a day which would never come.

Mab stood, her feet unwilling to take to the air. Her eyes were filled with the terrible vision of this child with a dagger in her heart, bleeding out the last beats of life upon the breast of Romeo. The tomb was so dark, and the vision filled with such hopelessness.

A single misstep and Mab knew this was their fate. A moment which stumbled instead of marching in lockstep, and death would be

Kate Danley

this young girl's groom.

And yet what choice did Mab have?

Mab left the home and walked to Juliet's garden, choosing to let the length of human footsteps forestall this fate, to have a few moments of respite before she set all upon a path of no return.

Chapter Thirty-Four

Queen Mab looked up at Juliet's window. She
knew she had to rise, to go within, and plant
the seeds of forgiveness in Juliet's dreams.
Let her love Paris, but she needed Juliet to
understand that the death which fell upon
Romeo's soul was done out of love, first to
protect Mab's own beloved Mercutio and then
to right the wrong of his friend's life cut too
short. Mab needed her to understand that if
he had not slain Juliet's cousin, it would have
been Romeo's life lost in the streets. Romeo
may be banished, but by his murderous hand,
he protected the House of Capulet. By killing
this cousin, he took the blame for Tybalt's

sins. It was Juliet's own father's kindness which beat within Romeo's veins, the same kindness which led Mab here in the garden at midnight praying she could bend a girl to mercy, to remember love when her love had been betrayed.

Bravely, Mab left behind the garden with its comforting smells of summer and ripening life. She flew to Juliet's balcony and stepped into her room.

It was here that gave her pause, for there was this daughter of Capulet entwined in a lover's embrace with the murderous Romeo. They slept, clinging to one another as if survivors of some terrible storm.

A silvery glint shone from Juliet's hand. A ring sat upon her third finger. Mab realized that she looked upon not just lovers, but a husband and wife in their marital bed. They were wed and bound together not just by heart, but by godly vows of fealty and devotion.

Mab sat down, in awe of a soul so young and yet so old. She herself had lived for centuries, and even so, shame for being made a fool made her try and destroy the world. Yet this young girl, this Juliet whose world had been destroyed, chose to follow the truth of her love, even if it meant welcoming in the enemy of her home.

Mab almost wept in both fear and joy. One step closer to the fate which she hoped to avert, but one step closer to happiness which could be forever theirs.

Queen Mab closed her eyes and leaned a hand upon Juliet's temple. "Dream, my child, of thy love. And welcome me into those dreams."

At once, Queen Mab stood upon a grassy knoll, a vast sky of blue behind her in contrast to the vivid green.

There Juliet sat with Romeo's head resting upon her lap. She stared down into a babbling brook in thoughtful revelry.

Queen Mab walked to Juliet's side and sat beside her.

The images that flashed through Juliet's mind were more beautiful than even the dreams Mab brought at night.

Dancers upon a floor.

Whispered words in a garden which brought a thrill with every memory.

The advance of a stolen kiss both foreign and familiar. How was it that two souls could cross a boundary that seemed a million leagues apart to close the gap and touch?

Queen Mab wondered how she ever could have thought these two nothing but playthings in her game with Faunus, to be pushed and pulled like chess pieces upon a board of black and white. Now... oh now... the feelings which beat in her breast with every flutter of her heart cast this child's life in such different colors. She must live. They both must live. And live happily! No longer could she destroy this girl to protect the House of Capulet. For, indeed, Mab had tasted love and knew of no sweeter drink. Mercutio had shown her the way and she would not deny its taste to another, for true love was rare enough. To push aside such a cup from the lips of one who had so few days to live on the earth? Juliet's heart was one with Romeo, and no matter what the size of the substitution, it would never fill the void he would leave behind. It would never heal the claw marks of his memory ripped away too soon.

No, the binding to Paris must be broken, Mab thought. As protector of the House of Capulet, it must not be. True, a marriage to Paris would keep the House of Capulet strong, but mortar made with blood left stains upon the foundation. Juliet was bound to Romeo, and if the world should end with such a joining, so be it. So be it. Far better than without. Days spent in love were worth an eternity without.

Queen Mab looked at Juliet and allowed peace to radiate off her being. "This is thy love?" she asked.

"Yes," Juliet nodded, gazing upon her husband Romeo. "But he must leave me for exile in Mantua, or else face execution by the prince's hand."

"This is of grave importance, my dear. I have looked into the future and seen that to be parted from him will mean certain death."

"Death?" Juliet whispered. The air became

dark and the sky began churning with the darkness of a storm.

"Death, my child," Queen Mab confirmed. "A domino of destruction will come if you are kept apart. Go with him! Though he his banished, leave not your husband's side. There is nothing more here for you if he is not with you. Travel with him to Mantua and live happily to the end of your days. Listen to this dream and remember!"

"I shall remember," said Juliet. "I shall."

Queen Mab waved her hand and once more the sky returned to turquoise blue.

"Do," Queen Mab whispered. "For it is in the forgetting of dreams that your fate will meet a terrible end."

And with that, the wind began to howl and sweep its way around Queen Mab, wrapping itself about her like a tornado. She shouted over the wind, "REMEMBER!"

Juliet sat up in bed, her heart pounding as Mab flew away to minister to the mind of another. The sun was barely risen and its weak rays broke through Juliet's curtained balcony. The birds outside were singing and their gentle music soothed and distracted her, reminding her that the terror that woke her was not real.

Still, Juliet was supposed to remember something... She tried to grasp the fading images. They were like water between her fingers. But then she remembered something about keeping her husband at her side.

Romeo was up and already dressing. He looked at her with such want and sadness, preparing for their long parting and his banishment. Rather than going to him to say goodbye, she tried to call him back to the bed. "Will you be gone already? It is not yet near day. It was the nightingale and not the lark that you heard. She sings in the pomegranate tree. Believe me, love, it was the nightingale..."

Chapter Thirty-Five

Queen Mab was waiting in Lord Capulet's bedchambers when he awoke. The sun upon her face should have filled Mab with astonishment and wonder. After a century without the touch of morning, she should have felt overwhelming joy to not fade with the dawn. To remain should have been a prized relished, and yet, there was no sense of victory. Instead, she tasted the bitter cost.

"Lord Capulet," she began as he stirred. "The day of your daughter's rebellion is upon us."

He looked at her like she was mad, a thief within his house, but she would not be silenced. She stepped forward, trying to will him to see the urgency of the matter. "Do not marry her to the County Paris. Your entire House lies upon the brink of destruction."

"Who are you?" he asked, clutching his coverlet with fear.

"I am Queen Mab, the protector of this House," she said with some confusion. "You saw me not but a few days ago at your masque. Is the human mind so forgetful and frail?"

"Nay, you do not have the face of the witch I know and Queen Mab could never leave her palace beyond the dawn."

"Nevertheless, I am she," Queen Mab went on, "And I come to you with words of dire warning. The prophesy I gave you over fifteen years ago is coming now to fruition. I beg you to heed my caution, no matter how discordant it may ring in your ears."

"Bah," said Lord Capulet, rising and getting his dressing gown. "Even if you are Queen Mab, why should I listen to a woman such as you? Protector of our House and yet you did not warn me against the death of my nephew."

"Tybalt's future was shielded from my eyes, but that does not prevent me from seeing what is to come. I am charged with preventing your House from fall. You must stop this wedding of your daughter to County Paris!"

"Shielded? You have failed, Queen Mab, and do not pretend it is otherwise. You warned me of my child's betrayal, yet abandoned my kinsman to a terrible end. Tybalt is dead and such sadness fills my House, it were better that my House was destroyed. This is your doing. I lay the blame squarely at your feet! You broke the promise you gave my forefathers and are a traitor to my kith and kin. I will not seek the guidance of one who can barely see the horizon. I have spoken with one wiser than you, one who has shown me the secrets of the future. By all that is precious to me, I swear that it shall be by the stars he sees, and not you, that I shall guide my barque."

Mab paused. "And who gave you these

comforting prophecies of which you speak?"

"A musician outside the Prince's palace who plays the pipes most cunningly."

Mab's blood froze in her veins realizing that Faunus was already playing his game so many steps ahead. She tried to warn, "I know this man and he cares not for your tender keep. He seeks instead prizes of adoration and greatness."

"Which I am happy to give if he keeps us more tenderly than we have been at your hand!"

"Do you not see! You must stop this marriage and reconcile with the Montagues! Welcome back this boy, Romeo! That is the only way you may both survive!"

And that was where Mab realized her error. Lord Capulet walked towards her, his cunning ways catching the unfortunate truth of her words.

"You say that heeding your words shall let us both live? What if I would happily sacrifice all to see that the House of Montague is forever shamed?"

"Be careful what you say you would happily

sacrifice, for I think you do not know the sorrow you are welcoming to your door."

"Perhaps I am not welcoming sorrow at all, but the joy of a marriage well made and the male grandchildren my daughter will bear."

"Your daughter will rebel, and in doing so, she spells your ruin," Mab pleaded.

"Then I will make certain that she has not the spirit or the strength to stand against my resolve."

Lord Capulet stormed out of the room towards Juliet's chambers, where shouts of anger already echoed down the hall.

Mab closed her eyes and willed that she might disappear from human view and become invisible to any gaze. Her cloud of smoke obeyed her and she faded soon to nothing. How strange to spend one hundred years longing to be in the flesh, and then her first day upon the earth, use her power to vanish once more. She followed Lord Capulet as he tore open the door to his daughter's room and strode inside. His daughter tearfully sat upon the bed as her mother and nurse looked upon her aghast.

"How now, Juliet? Are you still in tears? Still mourning for your cousin Tybalt? One would think your body has not the room for the sea of salt pouring from your eyes." He turned to Lady Capulet. "Wife? Have you delivered to her our decree and her happy betrothal to the County Paris?"

Lady Capulet replied bitterly, "Aye, sir. She gives you thanks, but will have no talk of marriage. I would the fool were married to her grave!"

Lord Capulet became deadly still. "Let me follow your meaning, wife. Does she not give us thanks? Is she so proud? Does she not consider herself blessed, unworthy as she is, that we have secured her a gentleman such as Paris to be her groom? Tell me again, wife, that I imagine these rebellions in a girl who should count herself lucky for the future we have brokered for her."

Juliet reached out to soothe him, to calm him with her words. "I am thankful and proud to have such parents who would seek to secure their daughter such security, but I am not thankful for what you have done. This marriage, no matter how good the intent is a hateful thing, even if when I know it was done with love. And so I thank you, but I must thank you not, and beg that you pardon me."

Lord Capulet raged, grabbing Juliet by the arm and throwing her to the floor. "You and your twisted words! How now! What is this? I thank you and I thank you not. Thank me no thankings nor proud me no prouds, but go with Paris to Saint Peter's Church on Thursday or I will drag you there myself!"

He pulled her up again and made for the door as if to take her to church that moment.

"Fie, fie! Are you mad?" asked Lady Capulet as she tried to pull her husband away. He raised his hand as if to strike her, then turned to the cowering Juliet.

His daughter begged, "Good father, I beseech you on my knees! Hear me with patience!"

But Lord Capulet, all kindness stolen from his heart and Mab's warning of this rebellion still fresh in his ears, would not listen her pleas. "Hang thee! Disobedient wretch! I tell thee what. Get thee to church on Thursday or never after look me in the face. Speak not, reply not, do not answer me! Wife, we thought ourselves blessed that God had given us but this only child, but now I see this one is one too much and that we have been cursed. Out on her!"

Her nurse tried to pull him away as he made to throw Juliet from their house. "God in heaven bless her! You are to blame, my lord!"

Lord Capulet turned towards her. "Hold your tongue!"

"May not one speak?"

Lady Capulet tried to calm him, warning. "You are too hot!"

"It makes me mad! Day, night, hour, tide, time, work, play, alone, in company, all this to have her matched, and now giving her a gentleman of noble parentage, youthful, with honorable parts, proportioned as any maiden would wish a man, and then have my daughter cry, 'I'll not wed! I cannot love! I am too young! I pray you, pardon me.' Go where you will Juliet, you shall not house with me. I do not jest. Thursday is near. You are mine and I give you to my friend. And if you spurn his friendly hand, you may hang, beg, starve, and die in the streets, for I will never acknowledge thee. Think on it."

Lord Capulet left, storming out of the room, leaving the tornado of his chaos in his wake.

Juliet cried, "Is there no pity that sees into the bottom of my grief?"

Mab heard and longed to reveal herself, to call upon her full might as the Queen of Dreams to demand that this marriage be put to an end, but she stopped, remembering Lord Capulet's anger and that she no longer held any power here. She thought of Juliet and how she used cunning to secure that which her heart desired. Perhaps in such strategy wisdom lay. Mab whispered in Juliet's ear to beg just for more time.

The young woman listened, for she turned to her mother and said, "O, my sweet mother, cast me not away! Delay this marriage for a month, a week! Or if you do not, make the bridal bed in that tomb where Tybalt lies."

Mab whispered to her mother to heed her daughter's words, but her mother would not be swayed.

"Talk not to me, for I'll not speak a word," said Lady Capulet, throwing up her hands and exiting. "Do as thou will, for I am done with thee."

Nothing was left but Juliet and her nurse. Juliet wept, "O God! O nurse, how shall this be prevented? My husband is here on earth. Counsel me! Have you not a word of joy? Some comfort, nurse?"

Her nurse gathered her in her arms, wiping the tears from her cheeks so wet. "Here it is, my girl. Romeo is banished and no one else knows how you are bound. He dares not come back to challenge for your hand, for it would mean his death. As things do stand, I think it best you marry this County Paris. Oh, he is a lovely gentleman to whom Romeo cannot compare. I think you shall be very happy in this second match, for it excels your first. You must think of Romeo as dead, for it is as good as if he were."

Leaning against her nurse's shoulder,

Juliet's voice was muffled. "Do you speak from your heart?"

"And from my soul, too," the nurse replied.

Juliet let the words linger in the air until the harsh vibration of their reality ceased. She took the emotions she had so freely shared and folded them quietly, tucking them into the corners of her soul so that she alone knew they were there. In that moment, Mab saw her turn from girl to woman.

Juliet rose coldly.

She turned away and spoke. "You have comforted me greatly and I see the path with which it is best I walk upon. Go in and tell my mother I am gone. Having displeased my father, I am to Friar Laurence's cell, to make confession and to be absolved."

"Marry, I will; and this is wisely done!" said the nurse. She toddled over and planted a kiss upon Juliet's temple, pleased her charge had come around. With a light heart, she left to do as she was bid.

Mab, however, watched and waited unseen.

Juliet looked after her nurse and waited until the door was closed before unleashing her storm. "O most wicked fiend! Praise for Paris with the same tongue which praised my Romeo above compare so many thousands of times? Go, counselor. You and my bosom henceforth shall be twain."

Juliet took down her cloak and placed it over her shoulders, hiding her face deep in its hood in case any passers might see the resolve in her eyes. She crept softly down the stairs, pausing by her father's study. Seeing he was not there, she went inside and opened the drawer of a chest. She removed a dagger and stared at it in her hand.

Mab grew chilled. The vision from fifteen years ago of this child with this naked blade plunged into her heart came back as if a conversation held only hours before. Surely a temporary separation was not worthy of such a permanent end. If only Juliet had heeded her warning and escaped to Mantua with her love. Mab looked at all the pieces of these hundred years, from the moment that bull was stolen to standing here in this study. It was as if every blunder, as if every tripping step moved them like a river towards this fate, and now the currents were almost too strong to fight against. But Mab vowed she would try. She whispered to Juliet that she have patience, that a solution was near if she only trust.

But Juliet had only half an ear for such tempered words. With her eyes fixed upon the blade, she murmured her resolve, "I'll to the friar who married us to hear his good reply. If I am powerless to forestall this fate, I shall always have the power to die."

Chapter Thirty-Six

Juliet lowered her hood as she stepped inside the chapel. As she turned the corner, she jumped back, startled by the face of one she had just met just two days ago at her father's masked ball. Only today, he did not wear his mask. No, he wore his face brazen and plain for any at all to see.

"Fair Juliet," said Paris. "Whither do you wander?"

"I confess to confession with my confessor," she spoke and tried to duck out of the way, but he was too fast. Twenty-one years at least and well acquainted with the excuses of women, her youth was no match for his guile.

"Juliet, there seems to be something changed about you. A spring to your step. A color to your cheeks."

"The day is quite warm, Cousin Paris. Now, if you will permit me to continue on my way, my nurse is awaiting my return and I must not delay."

"Let me stay and walk you home, gentle coz. The streets of Verona are scarce a place for a girl such as yourself to find yourself alone."

"Nay, not alone, but kept company by my silent prayers and reflections of holy love."

"So your mind does stray to thoughts of love? Tell me, Juliet, do those dreams of love contain room for one who stands before you?"

"Yesterday it would have depended upon the suitor," she replied, "But I am afraid that today, there is only room in my heart for one man."

Paris took her roughly by the arms and drew her close. "A word of kindness. A symbol of some tenderness and you would turn the grayest day to one of shining joy. Tell me, Juliet, have you any kindness in your heart which you might spare me?"

"No, sir, I do not," she replied as she struggled.

"Do not spurn me, for I love thee."

"I shall spurn thee, for I love thee not."

"A woman does not know her mind. Juliet, you will soon see me as a man worthy of being thy lord and master."

Juliet finally broke away and stepped back. She brushed back her hair which had come loose as she struggled. "Not until the sun does shine at night and the moon shines in day. No, Paris. I shall not have thee. Never shall I have thee."

"Juliet, I shall catch thee. The chase makes the victory taste only that much sweeter."

Friar Laurence cleared his throat.

Paris and Juliet turned to find him looking on. The old friar's gaze was cold and his godly presence a challenge to her delay.

"Fair Juliet, come thee to confession?" asked the Friar.

"Indeed, Father, until I was interrupted by

this man."

"Well, come now. My confessional is empty and God would like it if it were filled with thy words."

Juliet stepped resolutely past Paris, eyes as angry as a storm and followed the Friar into his inner sanctum.

The room was dark with only shadowed light from the slits in the narrow windows. Mab followed, watching Juliet's hands tremble as she removed her cloak.

"Oh shut the door!" Juliet wept, now in the safety of the Father's room. "And when you have done so, come weep with me. It is past hope, past cure, past help!"

Mab felt the young girl's pain as if it were her own. She knew and understood it as if she could feel the tears upon her own face. She lifted her fingers to her cheeks and, strangely, when she pulled away, they were wet. She could not fathom this feeling, this sense of understanding. It was almost as if Juliet had painted a dream for Mab and had welcomed her into her own world.

Mab wondered what this young woman's

life would be like if she had not stolen a father's kindness. Would this girl cling so tightly to her Romeo? If Mab had not interfered, would Juliet be happily wed with no hatred or prejudice to keep her from her love? Could this marriage have been one of joy and not of death?

The Friar spoke, trying to calm the child, to let her know that he understood her anguish, but as Mab's heart felt the pain as if a knife plunging through her heart, the words were nothing but sounds.

Indeed, Juliet removed a knife and spoke of a way in which to end this suffering, to enter a world of eternal dreams.

Mab looked upon the girl and the kernel of an idea sprang within her mind. As the Friar tried to comfort his young charge, Mab took out her wand and the empty vial that once held Lord Capulet's kindness. Mab's gift, her strength, was sleep. If the passage of time was too painful, perhaps time could pass without the girl having to endure its march. Perhaps Juliet could close her eyes and wake when her husband was near. Mab waved her wand and, as if writing a letter of amends for all the trials she caused this family, she placed the sweetest, deepest dreams inside the bottle.

She whispered in the good Friar's ear, "Tell her of a sleeping potion, of death which will lead to life."

Mab then placed it upon a table, as if such a draught was a home remedy that anyone might keep lying about.

The Friar's eyes lit up like he had realized the perfect plan. And so, as Mab whispered how the events must proceed, he unfolded a story for Juliet to take a vial which would cease her breath and still her heart, but she would be in sleep not death. And when she woke, he would ensure her Romeo was there to take her away.

Mab whispered, "Give her this ring and with it my protection."

The Friar handed it over, as if in a trance, and Juliet accepted it gladly. He wrote a letter to Romeo and placed it in the outgoing post, swearing to Juliet that his holy brothers would deliver it at once, and by tomorrow, her husband would be there.

While the Friar issued Juliet out the door, Mab took the letter and placed it in her pocket. She would see to it. Faunus had a way of leading notes astray.

As Juliet raised her hood, Mab could feel the girl's heart ablaze with love for the life she was to share with her Romeo. This lightness, this joy, gave Mab a moment of hope. She would play her part and in one night's dreams, Juliet would be reunited with her love. And in doing so, Mab prayed the balance would tip and once again the House of Montague be returned to its glory... and Mercutio to her arms.

Chapter Thirty-Seven

Lord Capulet dismissed two servants with their instructions to make ready for the wedding feast. He turned to see Juliet as she returned to the stronghold.

"How now, Juliet! Where have you been gadding about?" asked Lord Capulet.

Mab whispered in her ear, "Make peace. Tomorrow you shall be with your love and this kind deception will be a comfort when you are gone."

Juliet swallowed before bowing her head in shame-filled apology, being careful that her father could not see her eyes. "I have been to see Friar Laurence, to talk to him and in his wise ministrations, I have seen the wickedness of my disobedience and repent for my sin. I beg your pardon, Father, and from hereafter shall be ruled by you."

Lord Capulet's rage was at once dispelled, his anger replaced with joy. He called to a page and pointed out the way. "Go to Paris! Tell him that the wedding shall happen in the morning!"

Lord Capulet's booming voice drew Lady Capulet and the nurse. They seemed in wonder at this transformation.

Lord Capulet held out his hands to his wife and clasped hers with exuberance. Laughing he explained, "My daughter has seen the error of her ways!" He turned back to the page. "Go to the Friar and tell him to be here tomorrow to join these two in holy matrimony made the sweeter with a daughter's submission to her rightful place as wife."

Lady Capulet took her husband's arm. "No, not until Thursday. There is no need to proceed with such haste."

Lord Capulet shook his head at her reluctance, and spoke directly to the nurse so that there would be no mistake to his words. "Nurse, go with Juliet. We shall go to church tomorrow."

"We are not prepared for such a wedding. One more day and everything you might desire will be here," said his wife.

"It will all be well."

Juliet turned to her nurse and sweetly asked, "Will you help me to choose my wedding gown?"

Mab saw that her father's cruelty had found a place within this child, for it was not a wedding gown that the nurse would help to pick.

"Go to Juliet. Help to prepare her for tomorrow," Lord Capulet commanded the nurse. "I am off to County Paris to ready the bridegroom. My heart is wondrously light when I think of tomorrow, since this same wayward girl is so reclaimed."

Chapter Thirty-Eight

Juliet's gown was laid out upon the bed as darkness fell. It was green for fertility and the children Juliet would be expected to bear. But Mab reflected that it was as green as Mercutio's eyes, and hoped the color would not carry the cut of sadness for all the rest of her days.

"This is my most becoming dress?" Juliet asked her nurse.

"Aye! You shall be the most lovely bride in all of Verona." She came over and brushed back Juliet's hair. "You are so wise to bend to your father's wishes. It is a great showing for your upbringing and you bring honor to your house."

"It is lovely, made the more lovely with your hand to make the choice." Juliet said as she hugged her tight. "Now, please, leave me by myself tonight. I must have time to speak with my Maker, to ask His blessing, and make peace when I have been so full of sin."

The door opened and Lady Capulet came in. "Are you busy? Do you need my help?"

The look upon her face was as if she finally realized that by tomorrow, she would be letting her daughter go. But Juliet would not give her the affection that she seemed to crave. "No, madam. We have made our choices and now are to bed. Please leave me alone and let the nurse stay with you tonight. I am sure that you are quite in need of rest after all of the work you put into assembling these pieces to create tomorrow's picture of joy."

Lady Capulet nodded her head, as if somehow making light would make the painful truth less harsh. "Good night, then. Get to bed and rest. You will need it."

Lady Capulet kissed her upon the forehead, and the Nurse followed her out.

Juliet sat upon her bed. "Farewell! God knows when we shall meet again."

She removed the vial from her pocket and looked upon it. "A faint cold fear thrills through my veins, that almost freezes up the heat of life. I'll call them back again to comfort me. Nurse!" Juliet paused. "What should she do here? My dismal scene I needs must act alone."

"Nay, not alone," said Queen Mab. She stepped out of the shadows, allowing the moonlight in her veins to light the room.

Juliet stepped back. "Do I dream?"

"Always. But I appear to you in corporeal form to bear witness and stay by your side."

Juliet looked upon Mab. "You know what works I do?"

"Indeed, I am the one who planted those thoughts there and shall give you the strength to see them to the end."

"You seem a guardian angel, sent to me in this darkest hour."

Mab took the young girl's hand. "A

guardian am I, though an angel I am not, but I shall stay with you until the end."

Gently, she helped Juliet to stand and aided her change in her wedding attire. Mab brushed her hair smooth and prepared her for the moment that was to come. Juliet lifted the sleeping potion. "Come, vial."

The vial stopped on its way to her lips. Juliet looked at Mab. "What if this mixture do not work at all? Shall I be married then tomorrow morning?" She picked up her dagger. "No, no. This shall forbid it." She placed it by her bedside. "Lie thou there."

Mab did not dissuade her.

"What if it is a poison which the Friar gave to me to have me dead, lest in this marriage he be dishonored because he married me to Romeo? I fear it is."

"He has tried to be a holy man," Mab replied. "Do you think that he should deceive you to this end?"

"What if when I am laid into the tomb, I awake before Romeo comes to redeem me? Shall I be able to breathe? Shall I die, strangled by the poisoned air before Romeo comes? Or die of fright from the decaying bones of my own cousin Tybalt, who shall be lying there as my only company?"

"Do not fear," said Queen Mab. "For I shall guide your dreams and if you wake before your time, I shall be there to comfort thee."

Juliet nodded her head, all argument lost and the path clear, and lifted the vial to her lips. "Romeo, I come! This do I drink to thee."

Queen Mab tied her hair in faerie knots so that in the morning, the family would know who had been there and who was responsible for this death.

Chapter Thirty-Nine

Queen Mab sat with Juliet as her breath stilled in her chest, as the cold crept over her body. She sat as the sun rose and finally, as the sounds of the house moving filled her ears, she allowed herself to fade gently away.

She watched as the Nurse and Lady Capulet entered the room and threw back the heavy curtains. They scurried around in the excitement of the day, calling for spices and dates and quinces for the bridal feast, not noticing that the bride had not yet risen.

The strange kindness in Mab's breast wanted her to call out and tell them that the anguish they would soon feel was not a bitter as it might seem, but it was her memory of Mercutio and that not just Juliet and Romeo, but Mercutio's existence demanded silence be her friend.

Lord Capulet called up to the nurse, telling her to wake his daughter, crying out that the bridegroom was near.

Queen Mab held her tongue as the nurse shook young Juliet, merrily pronouncing, "You slug-a-bed! Marry, and amen, how sound is she asleep!"

Queen Mab kept still as realization slowly dawned upon the Nurse. Oh, but the Nurse's heart did break as she beheld the child she raised at her own bosom, the bond closer than even mother and child. As she noticed Juliet in her bridal attire, as the shock that she did not move settled in, as she cried, "Help, help! My lady's dead!"

Now Lady Capulet finally saw what her hand had done, all the days that were lost, all the years of not seeing. "O me, O me! My child, my only life, revive, look up, or I will die with thee! Help, help! Call help."

Lord Capulet stormed into the room,

thinking his child had merely relapsed into her earlier stubborn defiance. "Bring Juliet! Her lord is here!"

Neither Nurse nor Lady Capulet could answer words beyond. "She is dead! She is dead! She is dead!"

Lord Capulet looked as if they were speaking in foreign tongues, puzzled why his daughter could not rise. He felt her hand and spoke, "She is cold." He swept back her hair and straightened her gown, as if fixing the appearances might change the truth. "Death lies on her like an untimely frost upon the sweetest flower of all the field."

Friar Laurence and Paris entered in and Friar Laurence inquired, "Come, is the bride ready to go to church?"

His feigned innocence rang true.

"Ready to go, but never to return." Lord Capulet grabbed Paris's arm. "O son! The night before thy wedding day, Death hath lain with thy wife. There she lies, flower as she was, deflowered by him. Death is my son-in-law, Death is my heir. My daughter he hath wedded. I will die and leave him all—life, living, all is Death's."

Paris became as pale as if the life had been taken from him and not she. One after another, they seemed to almost play at grief, raising their voices to let the heavens know who had been injured the worst.

It was not until Friar Laurence raised his hands, chiding them, "Peace! For shame! She was a child of both you and heaven, and now heaven has taken her all. You sought her promotion, well, now she has been elevated to the clouds to sing among the angels. You weep now for her advancement? Dry your tears. Place rosemary upon this fair corpse, and take her to the church where she shall lie with her bridegroom in heaven."

Lord Capulet turned to the servants, which had gathered to see what horror caused the family to cry. He said, "All the things for this wedding, turn from white to black. The dance, to mourning, the cheer to burial feast, our bridal flowers serve for a buried corpse. All things, change them to the contrary."

Friar Laurence ushered the family away. "Sir, you go and, madam, go with him, and you, too, County Paris. Everyone prepare to follow this fair corpse unto her grave. The heavens have frowned upon you for some ill, move them no more by crossing their high will."

Lord Capulet paused at the doorway and murmured with regret, "Queen Mab warned me true."

Chapter Forty

"So you would rather her dead than wed, Queen Mab?" said Faunus. He was waiting outside of the home of the Capulets for her, listening and watching as the cries of the entire House turned from joy to weeping and sorrow. "I thought you sought to protect the Capulets, not ruin them."

She could see he was trying to glean her game. She kept the letter for Romeo from the Friar tucked within her pocket and cloaked herself in the now false face of her revenge. "If I cannot be with my love, no one shall."

"Death for a death for a death? You have blood on your hands, Mab."

"Aye, and I shall see more blood till the rivers run red."

Faunus shrugged his shoulders. "Do you think this will raise the House of Montague? To seat the Capulets so low that the Montagues seem upon a hill?"

"I will restore the House of Montague, Faunus, and I say that you shall not stop me."

"And I will see that it is truly destroyed. All that is yours shall be mine, and in this I shall rejoice."

"Why, Faunus? Why after all these centuries did you decide it was time to act?"

Faunus motioned to the sky. "My Queen, when you see the days fade one into the next, when you have tasted all the pleasures in your kingdom and then look out and see a world that you long for but know you shall never taste... well, an eternity of such longing will drive a person to madness."

"I would have shared it freely. If only you had not stolen my bull all those many years ago," she replied with soft truth.

"It was the only wise decision I ever made, for in stealing your bull, we are where we are now. This recent diversion has proved entertainment aplenty. Both you and I shall see this to the end. Indeed, the streets will run with blood, either yours or mine, Queen Mab. But one way or the other, it will end."

And with those words, Faunus was off leaping on cloven hooves towards Mantua. Queen Mab waved her rosewood wand and was at once the size of a dragonfly. She called a raven over, who swooped low and let her cling to the feathers of his back. "Away! We must fly!"

Over the farmlands they soared, past vineyards and flocks, but no matter how fast the bird's wings flapped, Faunus was still far ahead.

"For Mercutio," she thought. "I do this for Mercutio."

ଏୠଓ

Romeo walked the streets of Mantua when a servant he thought was Balthasar came into his presence. "How now, Balthasar! News from Verona! Do you have a letter from the

Friar? Have you word from Juliet? For my dreams seem to make me think that happy news is on its way to me. Nothing is foul when she fairs well!"

But it was not Balthasar. Faunus, cloaked in the illusion of this man, stammered and hung his head, as if what he shared gave him great pains. "She is dead. I saw her body laid out in the Capulet's vault myself. Forgive me for bringing such terrible news."

Romeo shook his head as if by shaking it he could turn the world on its axis and make time reverse. "I must leave. I must to Verona tonight. Hire me a horse! Get me a quill and parchment!"

"You cannot, my lord! If you are caught, it will mean your death!" Faunus spoke in false protest.

"Leave me to see what the cruel fates have spelled out in the stars for me. You are sure, no letters from the friar?"

"Not a one."

"No matter. Go. Prepare for my departure. We leave immediately."

Faunus gave a bow before going inside to

see to his master's command. While he could hide his horns and hooves, he could not hide the smile of glee and satisfaction from his face.

Alone, Romeo leaned against a wall for support, the grief causing his shoulders to heave in sorrow until, exhausted, they finally stilled.

"Juliet, I shall join you tonight. Though death may have parted us on this earth, in eternity we shall live side by side." Romeo lifted his eyes, and their glazed dullness seemed those of one who had already leaned into the Reaper's kiss. "There is an apothecary, a man of meager means who might be swayed by the weight of my purse."

Romeo stumbled blindly through the streets and stopped at a crumbling doorway, surrounded by withered plants in untended pots. Romeo called, his voice still rough from emotion, "What, ho! Apothecary!"

The man who came out was beggarly thin. His cheekbones were so sharp they could cut. His hair hung in ill-tended mats and his face was red from the long habit of tasting his own wares.

The apothecary called out, "Who calls so loud?"

"I see you are poor and I have forty ducats."

The apothecary looked at him with interest.

"Give me a dram of poison, one that will carry me off with the first drop and release me from this wretched life."

The apothecary shook his head and waved his hands to shoo Romeo away. "I may have such poisons, but the law would kill me should I give them to you."

"Are you so afraid to die? Your hunger shall kill you before the law shall rain upon your head. The world is not your friend nor is the world's law. The world's law will never make you rich." Romeo jingled his bag of coins. "So break the law and be not poor."

The apothecary's eyes lit up as he heard the clinking metal in Romeo's purse. His fingers rubbed, as if they could feel the silver and gold, and his lips whetted in desire. Slowly, the apothecary nodded his head as his soul made peace with his desperate wants. "My poverty, but not my will, consents."

Romeo replied, "Then I pay your poverty, and not your will."

The apothecary went inside and opened a drawer in his medicine chest. He unfolded a paper wrapped around a mound of innocent dust. "Put this in any liquid thing you will, and drink it off; and, if you had the strength of twenty men, it would dispatch you straight."

He poured it into a vial and handed it to Romeo.

Romeo, in turn, placed the heavy bag of ducats in the apothecary's hand gratefully, knowing that he himself would have no future use for it. "There is your gold. It is a worse poison to men's souls, doing more murders in this loathsome world than this compound that you may not sell. In fact, I have sold you poison; you, compassionate apothecary, have sold me none. Farewell." Romeo paused on his way out the door. "Buy yourself some food. Use these funds to hang meat upon your bones. I name you inheritor of my excess of days."

Romeo walked on, gripping the vial like a precious gem. "Come, cordial and not poison, go with me to Juliet's grave; for there must I use thee."

ᔥᕽ

Queen Mab came to Romeo's dwelling disguised in the robes of a layperson, the letter from Friar Laurence safely in her hand. She found the home deserted without a sign of life. Romeo and Faunus were gone.

Chapter Forty-One

The morning hours were close, but the sky was still dark. The funeral long since done, not a soul was left in the graveyard. The gate to the Capulet mausoleum where Juliet's body lay was left unlocked by the Friar in the hopes that Romeo would soon arrive.

It was not he, but another suitor, who made his way inside.

Paris took the torch and a small bouquet of flowers from his servant. "Keep your ear upon the ground and listen for any that might disturb me. Whistle if someone does approach. Give me these precious moments alone with the woman who should have been my bride."

The servant seemed only too happy to

depart and leave Paris in this gloomy place.

Paris tidied his straight, black hair nervously, as if to make himself presentable to this woman who never would care. He walked through the winding hallway, caskets placed into the walls and graves buried in the floors, until he reached the monument of Juliet's tomb. The marble sarcophagus sat in the center of the family crypt. Using a metal rod, he slid back the heavy lid. Paris shivered, promising the gods this violation was an act of love, not desecration. He put the delicate blossoms upon her bosom and bent over to kiss her brow. He whispered, "Death is but a passing shadow. A boundary where I may not tread. In living, and living well, I shall make each day a tribute to thee and mourn a life taken too soon."

He stirred, sensing that someone else had entered. Fear caused his pulse to race. He looked over his shoulder, unsure if he would find man or ghost.

It was neither.

It was an ethereal woman dressed in red velvet and gold. She swept towards him as if floating upon a cloud. The darkness seemed to greet her and return to her life and light.

"Who are you, beautiful woman?" spoke Paris, his eyes changing, roving over her body with hunger, the lady he came to mourn forgotten as if a dream.

Queen Mab stared at him strangely. "You do not recognize me?"

"Nay, gentlewoman. I have never set eyes upon you before."

Mab's mind was a whirl as she tried to guess Faunus's next move. This tomb should have been empty, but Paris was here just when Romeo might arrive. She might be a queen, but Faunus played at bishop—able to move in all directions, but only at an angle. She hoped she could protect the gentle pawn that lie asleep within the slab of stone.

"Let us say that we are here for the same reason," Mab replied.

Paris's vision seemed to dim, as if descending once again into another life. He turned back to Juliet. "To mourn the fall of the sweetest heart in the House of Capulet? If that is your purpose, then indeed, you find here a kindred soul."

Mab tilted her head in acknowledgement. "A man draws near, County Paris. A man who bears no harm towards thee, but comes tonight to make his peace. Depart from this place and let him be," she commanded.

Stricken, aware of the punishment if found opening a grave, Paris ran out to the churchyard. Mab followed after, exiting the door just as Romeo arrived with Balthasar. Rather than fleeing, Paris hid himself behind a tombstone to listen to what this man had to say. Mab crouched not far away, hoping he would continue home once Romeo was safely out of sight.

Romeo handed a note to his servant. "Take this letter. If you hold any affection in your heart towards me, Balthasar, see it delivered to my father."

Balthasar took it and placed it in his shirt front.

"Now, give me the torch. Do not meddle in the affairs to come, no matter what you witness." Seeing his servant's hesitation, Romeo clapped him on the shoulder and assured, "I enter to see Juliet, for upon her hand is a precious ring that I must retrieve. But I swear, if you come in to hinder me, I will strike you down and end thee. Do not doubt the truth of my words or my resolve."

Balthasar stumbled back from the force of Romeo's warning, then turned to run as fast as he could towards the House of Montague.

Romeo stepped forward and looked at the entrance of the mausoleum. He placed his hand upon the door, knowing what fate waited for him within when footsteps came from behind.

The sound of metal being removed from a sheath preceded Paris's voice. "Do you come here to defile the bodies of my love, Juliet, and her cousin, Tybalt? I shall apprehend you, Romeo, for only your death by the hangman's noose is the proper payment for the lives that you have purchased."

Dread filled Mab's heart. If she had known these would be Paris's words, she would have left him in the tomb to be surprised. It seemed as if every move she took to forestall the deaths to come only moved them one step closer. Oh, that she had never planted the dreams of love in this Paris, for they took too quickly to his mind and now, like a creeping vine, choked out all sense, and soon, all life.

But Romeo turned around and tried to warn him. "Tempt not a desperate man. Go. Leave me. Do not put another sin upon my head. I have come to take my own life and will not take yours."

"I do defy thy conjurations and apprehend thee for a felon here!"

"Will you provoke me?" Romeo pulled out his rapier. "Then have at thee, boy!"

He was met by Paris's on the first stroke. They sped about the courtyard, steel flashing as each played a deadly game.

"Put down your weapon!" Mab cried out, but neither paid her any heed.

Perhaps it was because their ears were filled with the whisperings of another.

A haunting tune played upon the pan pipes sang across the stones, trapping them in the dance, keeping time with the beats of their swords. Mab looked over. There Faunus sat dressed in the clothes of Balthasar, conducting this bloody tarantella.

"Let them leave, and in leaving live to see another day!" begged Queen Mab.

But still Faunus played on until the tune built to a crescendo, and with a final thrust, Romeo's sword found its home in Paris's broken heart.

Faunus stopped, laughing as Romeo crumpled, destroyed by what he had done.

"Why, Faunus?" Mab asked as she watched Romeo look disbelievingly upon the fallen Paris, coming to terms that he had killed again.

"The night shall be mine," Faunus whispered.

"Your days are just as dark. Why do you seek the shadows when the acts that play out best without light you commit just as proudly in the day?"

Romeo lifted Paris and took him into the

tomb.   Queen Mab tried to follow, but
Faunus stood in her way.

"The House of Montague and all its kin are
under my protection.   I will not have your
meddling," he taunted.

"You destroy his House and protect him
not! Let me save his life!"

Faunus grabbed Mab and threw her to the
floor. She got up, her anger fearsome and her
rage that of a queen.   She pointed her
rosewood wand and blasted Faunus, but with
light steps, he danced from the danger.   Mab
ran into the tomb.   The light of Romeo's
torch was close.   Juliet's tomb was within
sight. But then a terrible blow struck the back
of Mab's knees.   She fell, the stone floor
rattling her bones.   Faunus was at once upon
her back.   She knew no help would come as
he cloaked them both in magicked secrecy.
Her legs tangled in her skirts.   She struggled
and cried and tried to get away as she watched
Romeo take his beloved's hand.

Romeo wept.   "O my love!   My wife!
Death that has sucked the honey of your
breath has had no power yet upon your
beauty. You are not conquered.   Crimson is
still in your lips and cheeks.   Death's pale flag
is not there.   Ah, dear Juliet, why are you yet
so fair? Shall I believe that death is amorous

and keeps you here to be his paramour? I will not let him have you. I will stay with thee and never from this palace of dim night depart again. Here, here will I remain with the worms that are your chambermaids."

Mab drew upon her strength, upon the power of the daylight she had long since been denied, and willed that Juliet awake as if the sun was rising, that she abandon the dreams where she lay and see the morning was upon her.

But even as she spoke her magick, Faunus drove Juliet deeper into sleep so that she could not see as her husband withdrew a poisonous vial.

"Eyes, look your last! Arms, take your last embrace! And, lips, O you the doors of breath, seal with a righteous kiss a dateless bargain to engrossing death!" Romeo leaned over and kissed Juliet, his tears baptizing her before raising his glass. "Here's to my love!"

"No!" cried Mab. But her words would not be heard.

Romeo coughed. "O true apothecary! Thy drugs are quick. Thus, with a kiss, I die."

Mab ceased her fighting as Romeo exhaled his last and fell onto the floor.

Defeat rang as clearly as a church bell, its toll unmistakable and true. No hand upon the clapper would change that the hour had come.

Faunus laughed quietly in her ear. "The fall of Montague is complete."

Shuffling feet came from the entrance, the windowless dark masking the horrors from the sputtering light of Romeo's dying torch.

Friar Laurence stepped into the tomb, blind to the demigods that lay there among the dead. He tripped upon the hem of Mab's dress and cursed, "Have my old feet stumbled at graves? Who's there?"

Faunus replied in Balthasar's voice, "Here's one, a friend, and one that knows you well."

Friar Laurence replied with gladness, "Bliss be upon you! Tell me, good my friend, whose torch is that? It is so dim, I can barely see the Capulet's tomb."

"It belongs to my master and one you love. There he lies, one young Romeo."

Friar Laurence rushed forward, and then called back when Balthasar did not follow. "Come! Go with me into the vault!"

With a vise like grip, Faunus lifted Mab. She no longer had the spirit to struggle. He dragged her back and they retreated into the dark recesses of the tunnels, among the ancient graves of those who died when Faunus and Mab first began their game. "I dare not, sir. My master threatened me with death if I looked upon his intents."

"Stay then. I'll go alone."

Faunus looked down at Mab as he called out to the Friar. "I dreamt my master and another fought and that my master slew him."

The Friar ran forward, seeing the bloody streaks of Paris's crimson life upon the ground, his corpse discarded before Juliet's tomb. He saw the young Montague slumped lifelessly by his true love's grave. "Romeo!" he cried in anguish.

It was then that the fair Juliet stirred, her breath returning and her eyes fluttering to take in the world. As Juliet woke, stretching in her bed, the letter from the Friar for Romeo still burned in Mab's pocket.

Juliet turned to the Friar and asked, "Where is my love? Where is my Romeo?"

The Friar did not answer, instead looked at the entrance in fright. "I hear a noise! Come! A greater power than we can contradict has thwarted our intentions. It was written in the stars that you two may only be together in dreams. Come away!"

He tried to drag Juliet from her tomb, but she would not go, so Friar Laurence pointed to the shapes strewn throughout the room. "Your husband is beside you and lies there dead. And Paris, too. Come. I shall take you to a convent where you may be hidden from harm and kept safe for the rest of your days."

Mab stirred from her state, remembering the vision of a knife in Juliet's chest. She threw Faunus off her and made another desperate leap to reach the tomb, but he captured her up again, clamping his hand over her so that she could not speak or move.

The Friar heard the noise, though, and said, "We dare no longer stay."

Juliet pushed his helping hand away. "Go. Get thee hence. I shall not depart."

Friar Laurence scurried off, leaving Juliet with none but the dead to keep her company.

Juliet climbed out of her stone casket and knelt by the body of her husband. Gently, she let her fingertips memorize the features of her beloved, ran her fingers through his hair of gold, over his skin so pale and still. She then looked down and saw the means by which he had met his end. "What's here? A cup closed in my true love's hand? Poison, I see, hath been his timeless end." She pressed her body close to him, clasping his head to her heart, as the tears of grief fell from her eyes. "You have drunk all and left no friendly drop to help me after? I will kiss thy lips. Perhaps some poison yet does hang on them." Her mouth lingered upon his hungrily, knowing this would be her last taste, before observing in sad wonder, "Thy lips are warm."

A watchman called from outside the tomb. "Lead, boy! Which way?"

Juliet looked back in fear, knowing that if they found her, they would force her away. "Yea, noise? Then I'll be brief." She pulled a knife from Romeo's belt and held it to her breast. "O happy dagger! This is thy sheath!"

Mab saw now that all her power as queen was nothing compared to the will of the gods. She was a fool to think she could ferry these children away from the fate written in the stars. Mab wept as the vision she had seen for fifteen years came to pass. Juliet took the dagger and, without hesitation, she stabbed it straight into her heart. She gasped as the blood poured out. She leaned against Romeo as if for strength, so that his touch would be the last sensation she ever would know. She looked at her husband, at her true love's face and smiled at him through the pain. "There rust, and let me die."

As all fell to silence, Faunus whispered in Mab's ear, "A century's old game has finally come to an end. And that note you carry undelivered is all the proof that Juno needs. You are guilty of this destruction. Your weapon? A simple slip of paper which could have prevented this fall. One hundred years of planning and I have finally won, Queen Mab."

He removed his hand from her mouth. Mab asked only one question. "But why?"

"Are you too besotted to see? Then the secret, Queen Mab: your rule and kingdom are merely the spoils of war as I march to take my place at Jupiter's side. But even ruling the heavens does not compare to the true victory I seek: your complete and utter destruction. For I despise thee."

Queen Mab wept no more. "I know."

Faunus looked at her strangely.

Unafraid, strong, Queen Mab met his eyes.

Paris's page ran into the room, leading the way for Prince Escales, followed by Lord and Lady Capulet, and the watchman.

The prince turned to the page. "What misadventure is so early up, that calls our person from our morning's rest?"

Lord Capulet asked him, "What should it be that they so shriek abroad?"

Lady Capulet said, "The people in the street cry Romeo, some Juliet, and some Paris; and all run with open outcry toward our monument."

The watchman pointed. "Sovereign, here lies the County Paris slain; and Romeo dead;

and Juliet, dead before, warm and new killed."

The prince commanded, "Search, seek, and know how this foul murder comes."

Faunus rose, releasing Queen Mab. "My role in this play is not quite done. Watch and see the final act."

Faunus picked up the discarded iron which Paris had brought into the tomb and stepped before the watchman as he ran about. The watchman grabbed Faunus, now Bathasar, by the arm and thrust him forward into the light. "We found him with instruments fit to open these dead men's tombs."

It was at that moment that Lord Capulet fell to his knees. "O heavens! O wife, look how our daughter bleeds!"

Shuffling feet echoed in the chamber and Lord Montague, a man who looked like he could bear no more, entered.

The prince took his arm to brace the tottering man. "Montague, you come alone?"

Lord Montague shook his head. "Alas, my liege, my wife is dead tonight. Grief of my son's exile has stopped her breath. What further woe conspires against me?"

"Look, and you shall see."

Trembling and broken, Lord Montague wailed as he saw his son. He bent down and clutched him to his chest. "Oh unschooled child. Have you no manners? To push before your father to the grave?"

The prince placed his hand upon his shoulder. "Seal up the mouth of outrage for a while. Let us learn what has happened here. Bring forth the parties of suspicion."

Another watchman entered the tomb with Friar Laurence as his prisoner. Bravely, the Friar stepped forward and stated, "I am the one to blame."

The good holy man then went to explain the tale of these two lovers, husband and wife, and how two House's hate drove them to such ends. He spoke of their meeting and marriage, their happy plans, and how the fates took hold of this star-crossed love and chose to unite them in the world beyond since the world here was unworthy of their unity.

The prince looked at the Capulets and Montagues and said, "See what a scourge is laid upon your hate? All are punished."

The last of Lord Capulet's pride was destroyed, and with the pride, the fall, and so the House of Capulet crumbled. The contract was broken and Mab had failed. That which bound her to the Capulets was gone.

And with the breaking, so returned the price that Lord Capulet had paid in full. From Mab's body, she felt his kindness pour, returning to his spirit a gift without measure.

It settled down upon him like the embrace of a lover who could find a hideous faerie queen beautiful, wrapped itself about him like a cold queen who had found herself able to love unconditionally and be loved in return.

Lord Capulet reached out to his enemy and said, "O brother Montague, give me thy hand. It is my daughter's dowry, no more can I command."

And his enemy, overrun with grief looked at Lord Capulet and felt the kindness which had been so long away, felt that seed of an ancient friendship which was thought to have been destroyed. In the grieving heart of a phoenix's ashes, that kindness found its root and Lord Montague replied, "But I can give thee more. I will raise her statue in pure gold. For as long as Verona lives, there shall be no woman known more true and faithful as this, our Juliet."

The tears streamed down the two fathers' cheeks, Lord Capulet wrapped his hand around his sworn enemy's and declared, "As rich shall Romeo's statue be and by his lady's lie. And from this day forth, it shall be known that these two loves were terrible sacrifices of our enmity!"

The Prince spoke the words that their

heavy hearts would carry to the end of their days. "A glooming peace this morning brings. The sun, for sorrow, will not show his head. Go to talk more of these sad things, for never was a story of more woe than this of Juliet and her Romeo."

Under the Prince's watchful eye, arm-in-arm, the two families left the tomb, united after a century apart, in their grief.

Strangely, though, the Prince did not leave. Indeed, he still stood, and when the last footstep was heard upon the stone, he looked upon Mab with eyes that pierced the veil of dreams and nodded. "And so both the House of Montague and Capulet rise to greatness once again."

The prince's trappings faded away and he turned into a goddess with terra cotta curls.

Balthasar's disguise faded, too, leaving Faunus standing there enraged. He brayed at Juno, "Rise to greatness once again? Goddess Juno, call justice down upon Mab's head! She cannot be allowed to abide in this fair city in light or dark!"

"I shall not abide two hearts not in love to be bound in unholy matrimony to play out the politics of a fallen House!" Queen Mab replied in deadly earnest. "Better to be in death's embrace than to be confined to the embrace of a love that is not true."

"You shall rue the day that you let these mortals die! Goddess Juno, the blood sacrifice of the Montagues is before thee, sinned by Romeo's own hand while Queen Mab stole a letter which would have prevented the deaths this day. I swore to protect the House of Montague and Queen Mab kept secret the one thing which would have stayed these terrible acts."

Juno looked at Faunus as her peacock circled his feet. "Sworn to protect the House of Montague? Indeed, I saw you take actions to guarantee its ruin, even as this woman here fought for my followers' survival. No, Faunus. You shall not rule night or day. From this moment forth, whenever man, woman, or child look upon your cloven hooves and horns, they shall see the true nature of your evil and know to run from your seduction. And so I say to you, Faunus, run! For I will set a host upon thee to chase thee to the ends of the earth. Run!"

And so the demigod Faunus fell. And he ran, ran as fast as he could, for Juno did not jest.

When the last sound of his hooves faded in the distance, Juno turned to Mab and whispered, "Continue."

The world became cold as Queen Mab closed her eyes, as she ended this dream and woke in the frozen truth of her prison, in her world that was not Verona. The mausoleum with its carnage, with the blood that poured from dear Juliet's breast, faded and disappeared. In its place, Juliet still rested within her slab of stone and Romeo slept quietly beside her casket. All was icy and white. Queen Mab fell, exhausted, to the floor as she released the last of the false dream she had created, a dream which had shielded them all.

Romeo's eyes fluttered and he murmured, " I dreamt my lady came and found me dead-- Strange dream, that gives a dead man leave to think!—and breathed such life with kisses in my lips that I revived and was an emperor. Ah me! How sweet is love itself possessed, when but love's shadows are so rich in joy!" He slowly took in his surroundings and then looked at Queen Mab with desperation and despair. "Why did you wake me from my eternal sleep? Why have you condemned me to a lifetime on this earth when my spirit wishes no more than to lift itself from this mortal form? Are you an angel come to seek revenge for this hand which sinned against nature so?"

"Nay, gentle Romeo," Queen Mab replied. "Indeed, I have brought you back from death and lifted the veil of dreams so that you may be united in love with your Juliet."

Romeo looked at Mab in confusion. "But she lies here dead?"

"Nay, look closer."

Romeo stood and walked over to Juliet's uncovered tomb. He brushed back her hair from her neck. Slowly, ever so slowly, did her pulse beat in her throat.

"She lives," he whispered with tears in his eyes.

"She lives," replied Queen Mab. "And her life is repayment for all the ill-gotten deeds I have done. Rejoice, gentle Romeo."

He stroked Juliet's cheek and his face was the first sight that her eyes gazed upon, as the good Friar had promised. Tearfully, they joined.

"You are here," Juliet replied.

"I should not be," spoke Romeo, "for if not for the intercession of this woman, I would not." Romeo looked up from his love just long enough to try and find out who their savior was. He turned to Mab. "How did this all come about?" Slowly, comprehension began to dawn as Romeo remembered where they had met before. "You! You were the hooded apothecary who gave me the poison."

"True, I was the apothecary, but the only draught I gave you was to sleep as true as your true love slept."

Mab walked over to Juliet's hand and removed the ring Friar Laurence had passed along. And with its removal, the air shimmered, and the mausoleum door opened to the warm Italian countryside laying outside in wait.

"You shall be safe," said Queen Mab to the young couple. "If these things had not come to pass, your family would have split you asunder. But now you are free to live your lives and grow old together. Do so. Live and be happy and be young until you are old, and when you are old, hold each other close and remember all that you have would have been lost on this fateful day. Treasure every moment, for today it could have been gone."

But before Romeo and Juliet could go on to the happy destiny that lay in wait for them, a figure emerged from this doorway of light.

Mab's heart pounded, disbelieving. Her legs gave way and she could no longer stand. A gasping sob wracked her chest.

Romeo paled as he recognized the man. "You are a ghost! A man I know to be dead! And yet, you are here before me. What magic brings you thus?"

Mercutio, whole and strong, shook his head. "Dead I am, but alive still, brought back to tend the garden of the dreamer's mind. Goddess Juno has explained to me." He gripped Romeo's arm, his friend's face awash with grief and hope. Mercutio promised him, "I leave you not again. You shall see me as the consort to a queen when you sleep, and know me when inspiration strikes at day. Together with my beloved, we have a great and blessed duty to share."

Mercutio walked over. He knelt and gently gathered Mab up in his embrace. He pushed the drenched tendrils from her face, and tenderly kissed her exhausted eyelids.

"Who is this fair lady?" asked Romeo in wonder.

"She is the Queen of Dreams," said Mercutio, rocking her softly. "My beautiful, beautiful queen."

Mab leaned against the might of his heart. The heat and power of his life seemed never to have left him. Death never seemed to have touched him with its chill. Mercutio was here. Her Mercutio was here.

"Will you have me, lady?" he asked, his eyes of sea green searching hers for her reply. "What dreams we shall have…"

She gave her answer in her kiss.

Their lips finally parted, but neither let go. Mercutio whispered, "You are no longer cold, my queen."

Juno laughed. "Never more, Queen Mab, shall children scream in fright when you come to visit them half awake and half in dreams. No more shall those around you recoil from your hideous nature. As I said that day so many years ago, this was a prison of your own making. And now it is a prison no more."

The cold and ice of Mab's world swiftly began to turn. It melted and disappeared like nightly visions as the sleeper wakes. Romeo and Juliet faded, with tender smiles upon their lips as they made their final bow. The walls of the tomb opened to blue skies, to soft drifting clouds. The stone replaced with rolling hills and sparkling grapes, of bird song and babbling brooks. The prison that had held her for one hundred years, exploded, replaced with a world of golden light. She looked at Mercutio, and she was warmed to her very bones.

Yes, the House of Capulet fell, along with the House of Montague, and with their destruction, they rose again, forever being as one. It was just what her basin had foretold. But she did not know that this fall and rebirth was also meant for her.

She took her true love's hand and stepped forward into that place she had thought forever barred. She was trapped in the darkness and cold no more, a prison that she had thought true was nothing more than but a dream.

As Mercutio looked down softly at her, holding his place at her side, she realized the dreams she once thought the sweetest tasted nothing in compare to the life that was about to begin.

For Mab was finally awake.

ACKNOWLEDGEMENTS

One of my earliest memories is sitting with my mom as she read *A Midsummer Night's Dream* aloud to me. You read a million books to your children, and isn't funny the ones that will later go on to shape their life? My mom was a Shakespearean scholar, a feat which, to this day, fills me with awe and admiration.

This book, *Queen Mab*, led me on an amazing journey. From the Folger to Stratford to The Globe in London as I hunted down productions, old shows on VHS, and obscure printings of *Romeo & Juliet*. My great-grandparents were from Verona and it was a delight to pour through the research and learn more about my own roots. Eventually, though, I realized I needed to expand my Shakespearean knowledge so that the scholars wouldn't set me on fire for blasphemy. To this, I owe a debt of gratitude to the William Geer Theatricum Botanicum and their Shakespeare Intensive, taught by (in alphabetical order) Susan Angelo, Madeleine Dahm, Sandi Massie, Ellen Geer, Willow Geer, Armin Shimerman, Kristof Konrad, Melora Marshall, and Lori Anne Ferrell, and the Impro Theater Shakespeare Improvisation class (yes, I can now improvise an apostrophe for you any time you'd like, and sometimes even in iambic pentameter) taught by Brian Lohman.

But most of all, thank you to the Bard for the eternity found in his words.

Support your local theater.

ABOUT THE AUTHOR

Kate Danley is a twenty-five year veteran of stage and screen with a B.S. in theatre from Towson University. She was one of four students to be named a Maryland Distinguished Scholar in the Arts.

Her debut novel, *The Woodcutter*, was honored with the Garcia Award for the Best Fiction Book of the Year, the 1st Place Fantasy Book in the Reader Views Literary Awards, and the winner of the Sci-Fi/Fantasy category in the Next Generation Indie Book Awards. *Queen Mab* won the McDougall Previews Award for Best Fantasy Book of the Year

Her plays have been produced in New York, Bath, Los Angeles, Houston, Baltimore, Chicago, and Seattle. Her screenplay *Fairy Blood* won 1st Place in the Breckenridge Festival of Film Screenwriting Competition in the Action/Adventure Category and her screenplay *American Privateer* was a 2nd Round Choice in the Carl Sautter Memorial Screenwriting Competition.

Her projects *The Playhouse, Dog Days, Sock Zombie, SuperPout*, and *Sports Scents* can be seen in festivals and on the internet. She trained in on-camera puppetry with Mr. Snuffleupagus and played the head of a 20-foot dinosaur on an NBC pilot. She has over 300+ film, theatre, and television credits to her name.

She lost on Hollywood Squares.

Sign up for her newsletter at
www.katedanley.com

DID YOU LIKE WHAT YOU READ?

- Tell your friends!

- Leave a nice review at your favorite online book retailer

- Sign up for the Kate Danley newsletter at www.katedanley.com to hear about upcoming releases and sales

Thank you!

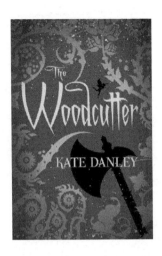

THE WOODCUTTER

Deep within the Wood, a young woman lies dead. No mark on her body. No trace of her murderer. Only her chipped glass slippers hint at her identity.

The Woodcutter, keeper of the peace between the Twelve Kingdoms of Man and the Realm of the Faerie, must find the maiden's killer before others share her fate.

But quickly he finds that one murdered maiden is not the only nefarious mystery afoot: one of Odin's hellhounds has escaped, a sinister mansion appears where it shouldn't, a pixie dust drug trade runs rampant, and more young girls go missing. Looming in the shadows is the malevolent, power-hungry queen, and she will stop at nothing to destroy the Twelve Kingdoms and annihilate the Royal Fae…unless the Woodcutter can outmaneuver her and save the gentle souls of the Wood.

Blending magic, heart-pounding suspense, and a dash of folklore, The Woodcutter is an extraordinary retelling of the realm of fairy tales.

Available from 47North

Made in the USA
Lexington, KY
20 November 2016